THIS ONE'S A REAL
MOTHERFUCKER, SIX...

"... dazzling art and an interesting psychological drama"

– Bloody-Disgusting.com

"This comic is a really great read, like the kind of stuff we used to get from *Preacher*, *Y: The Last Man*, and *Transmetropolitan*."

– IGN.com

"Kowalski's art continues to impress, using light and shadow as his weapons, just as much as the understated colour spectrum that has become a signature of the series so far. *Sex* is a slow-builder, and one that we suspect will ultimately reward a reader with stamina and longevity."

– Behind the Panels

"... the art, the color, the textures, or the writing, everything about this comic is good and when it all comes together it is something amazing."

– Speak Geeky To Me

"... a great read with great characters who are all a bit off and deeply complex. 5/5 stars."

– Unleash the Fanboy

"Do yourselves a favor and just give it a chance, better yet, read it with your significant other. Do it. Come on. You know you want to."

– Ket's Comics

"... under the radar but sure to be a classic."

– Geeked Out Nation

"Joe Casey and Piotr Kowalski have create a stylish look at an often overlooked part of the superhero genre."

– Comic Book Resource

".. the long-sought-after 'HBO of Superheroes' – a long term, adult-oriente story that tries to say something not just about the genre but about society."

– Sequart Organizatio

"... another sharp, twisted take on superhero clichés."

– Publishers Weekl

"... taps into an area that is rarely given light in the comic world."

– Comic Bastard

"*Sex* continues to keep you guessing at what it's got up its sleeve next... worth the tension and anticipation."

– Unleash the Fanbo

"... the maturity extends to Piotr Kowalski's art, which is incredible for an artist of his relative level of experience in comics."

– Multiversity Comic

"*Sex* is probably one of his finest yet."

– All-Comi

"As creators, what Kowalski, Casey and Simpson love is pillow talk, which is perfect for a comic called *Sex*."

– Comics Bulleti

"Joe Casey has done a lot of thoughtful and provocative work in the comics industry, but *Sex* is probably one of his finest yet."

– All-Comic

"... gorgeous artwork from Kowalski, who ensures that the reader inhabits the sticky work of Saturn City."

– Behind the Panels

"... anyone who approaches *Sex* with an open mind and a willingness to take their time with it is much more likely to have a fulfilling experience than those who try to rush it."

– Comic Bastards

"... if you miss the honed sense of danger you got when reading *The Dark Knight Returns*, *Watchmen* and *American Flagg*! it might be time for you to check out the Image comic, *Sex*."

– Comics Alliance

"*Sex* pulls off a great feat by embracing familiar elements from past famous works while feeling wholly unique."

– IGN.com

"... an adult comic in the truest sense in that it wants to approach the subject of sex in an actually adult manner, which is very rare to find in comics."

– Front Towards Gamer

"The genius of *Sex* is how those subplots continue to evolve and morph into more story without reaching a 'conclusion' because that's not what this book, or storytelling in a general sense, is about."

– Nothing But Comics

"... provides the graphic nudity that its title suggests, but also keenly takes on the interactions among big business, the media, political power players, gang bosses and former superheroes and villains."

– Big Glasgow Comic Page

"... it will leave you wanting more, another itch you can't wait to scratch."

– Nerdlocker.com

"*Sex* is extremely interesting and quite dynamic."

– Rhymes With Geek

"Casey has written a vast and layered tale that has been as entertaining as it has been dirty."

– Comic Bastards

"... a labor of love that is overflowing with pathos, humor, and humanity."

– Multiversity Comics

"... showcases Saturn City as a living breathing entity full of many moving parts and players."

– Comics Bulletin

BOOK SIX:

ORLD HUNGER

www.manofaction.tv

SEX BOOK SIX: WORLD HUNGER

First printing. April 2019.

Published by Image Comics, Inc.

Office of publication: 2701 NW Vaughn St., Suite 780, Portland, OR 97210.

Printed in the USA.

For information regarding the CPSIA on this printed material call: 203-595-3636.

For international rights, contact: foreignlicensing@imagecomics.com

ISBN: 978-1-5343-0877-0

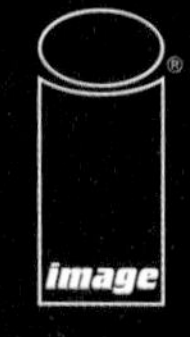

JOE CASEY WRITER
PIOTR KOWALSKI ARTIST
BRAD SIMPSON COLORIST
RUS WOOTON LETTERER
SONIA HARRIS GRAPHIC DESIGNER & COVER ARTIST

WHO IS IN SEX?

SIMON COOKE
Rich. Retired. Repressed.

ANNABELLE LAGRAVENESE
Club owner. Catty. Confident.

KEENAN WADE
Courageous. Undaunted. Infiltrator.

QUINN
Mentor. Puppet master. Deceased.

WARREN AZOFF
Lawyer. Confidant. Pimpmeister.

JULIETTE JEMAS
Journalist. Single. Single-minded.

MASAI
Break. Boss. Bad ass.

LORRAINE BAINES
"Larry". Cooke Company executive. Capable.

THE ALPHA BROS.
Cha Cha & Dolph. Criminal. Ambiguous.

THE OLD MAN
Gangster. Weary. Deceased.

ELLIOT K. BARNES
Loyal employee. Awkward. Unhinged?

VIZ IBN ZIYAD
Unknowable. Manipulator. Enigma.

THE PRANK ADDICT
Remnant. Hospitalized. Faking amnesia.

RAYMOND & REGGIE
Bodyguards. Bruisers. Eyeballs.

VERNITA
Girlfriend. Suspicious. Scared.

ALBERT EISENHOWER
Operator. Intel nexus. Toothless.

THE BONE COLLECTOR
Seductive. Strange. Saturn's Most Wanted.

SKYSCRAPER
Break muscle. Big. Befuddled.

NEW BABY
Name unknown. Of questionable lineage.

CHAPTER THIRTY-FIVE

CAUTION: MOVING PARTS

CHAPTER THIRTY-FIVE

CAUTION: MOVING PARTS

SO HERE'S WHERE I'M AT. BEAR WITH ME.
YOU KNOW I'VE ALWAYS SAID THERE WAS SOMETHING ABOUT SIMON COOKE. THAT HE'S MORE THAN YOUR AVERAGE MILLIONAIRE CEO.
WE KNOW THAT MOST OF HIS SOCIAL ACTIVITIES ARE A COMPLETE RUSE. BUT WHY? WHY WOULD HE FAKE AN ENTIRE LIFESTYLE?
WELL, I THINK I KNOW WHY.
OKAY, YOU'RE NOT SAYING ANYTHING. IT'S WEIRDING ME OUT.
SORRY. I WAS LISTENING.
SOMETIMES I FORGET I'M ACTUALLY HERE IN THE ROOM WITH YOU.
VERY FUNNY, MITCH.
HAVEN'T I INDULGED YOU ON THIS STORY?
HAVEN'T I STRETCHED THE DEFINITION OF "INVESTIGATIVE JOURNALISM" TO RIDICULOUS DEGREES IN ORDER TO ACCOMMODATE YOU?
NOW, AS YOUR EDITOR, OBVIOUSLY I'M EXCITED TO HEAR WHATEVER YOU'VE COME UP WITH. IT'S CERTAINLY BEEN LONG ENOUGH.
SO DON'T BURY THE LEDE, JEMAS. YOU'RE BETTER THAN THAT.
WELL, LET'S JUST SAY THAT SIMON COOKE IS TURNING OUT TO BE A LOT MORE DANGEROUS THAN I EVER IMAGINED...
... HE'S BEING RECRUITED INTO THE ROTHCHILD GROUP.

NO SHIT...
... SO IT TURNS OUT HE'S JUST ANOTHER MEGALOMANIAC WHO WANTS TO RUN THE WORLD.
WELL, THAT'S THE *THING*, MITCH. I'M NOT SO SURE.
FROM WHAT I'VE *GATHERED* ON HIM, THE ROTHCHILDREN SHOULDN'T BE HIS SCENE *AT ALL*.
BUT THAT, IN ITSELF, GETS MY SPIDER-SENSE TINGLING...

THEY'RE HAVING ONE OF THEIR SUPER-SECRET *MEETINGS*. IN *AUSTRIA*, THIS TIME. AND I THINK SIMON COOKE IS GOING TO BE THERE.
AND EVEN THOUGH I HAVE NO IDEA *WHY*, THAT'S ONE HELL OF AN *ONION* TO PEEL.

EITHER WAY, IT'LL BE A SENTINEL *EXCLUSIVE*.

OKAY, JEMAS. I'M STILL ON BOARD.
BUT I CAN'T SEND YOU ALL THE WAY TO AUSTRIA. NOT OFFICIALLY, ANYWAY. THOSE ROTHCHILDREN... I DON'T WANT TO POKE THAT BEAR UNLESS YOU'VE GOT YOUR STORY *COLD*.

I WOULDN'T HAVE IT ANY OTHER WAY, MITCH.
DON'T WORRY. I'LL FIND MY *OWN* WAY OVER THERE.
THIS CITY ALWAYS PROVIDES.

SATURN CITY;
TODAY:

KEENAN WADE! WHAT THE FUCK ARE YOU DOING?!
I HAVEN'T SEEN YOU FOR DAYS --
I KNOW, BABE. AND I MISS THE SHIT OUTTA YOU...

... BUT I'VE BEEN STAKING OUT SKYSCRAPER'S CRIB, WAITING FOR HIM TO SHOW HIS FACE...!
EVER SINCE HE BAILED WITH SHEILA'S BABY, I DON'T KNOW WHAT HE'S UP TO!
I JUST DON'T WANT HIM GETTING INTO MORE TROUBLE...

... SO FAR I'VE HAD ZERO LUCK.
YEAH, YOU GOT A BIG HEART, BABY. BUT COME ON --

-- WHAT DOES ANY OF THAT HAVE TO DO WITH YOU?!
HEY, SKY'S MY BOY. AND I KNOW HE'S JUST HAVING A ROUGH TIME OF IT.
ANYWAY, I GOTTA PEEL OFF NOW. GOT ANOTHER MEETING WITH THE BIG BAD...

IT'S ALL HAPPENING, MOTHER-FUCKER.
Masai. King of the Breaks. And he's at the peak of his king shit attitude...

...not that he can't ...ack it up, big time.
ONLY ONE THING STOPPING US FROM FINALLY RUNNING THIS CITY.
AT THE NETWORK LEVEL, ANYWAY.
THE SKINS.
IT'S TIME TO BUST THEM UP, Y'DIG?
I DIG.
'BOUT TIME, TOO.

I HEARD THAT.
I'll give him this... he's a goddamn black belt in multitasking.
It's like he's carved out of stone.
Immovable. Unbreakable. Power personified.

I never expected I'd end up this close to the fire so soon.
YOU AND I BOTH KNOW THAT BULLCHUCK AIN'T BEEN ABLE TO DO SHIT WHILE WE ROLL INTO HIS TERRITORIES.
HE'S A PAPER CHAMPION. BUT HIS SOLDIERS CAN'T AFFORD TO ADMIT THAT.
HE'S A SYMBOL. AND SYMBOLS MATTER.
TAKE DOWN THE SYMBOL, THEY'LL HAVE NOTHING LEFT TO STAND FOR. THEY'LL BE IN COMPLETE DISARRAY. AND THAT'S WHERE WE WANT 'EM.
WE'RE NOT LIKE THAT, ARE WE? REAL LEADERSHIP. REAL AUTHORITY.
YOU'VE SEEN IT, WADE. WITH YOUR OWN EYES. SOMEONE COMES AROUND TO TAKE ME OUT...
... THEY'LL LEARN THE HARD WAY HOW I GOT HERE IN THE FIRST PLACE.
THIS IS THE MOMENT WHEN SATURN CITY BECOMES OUR CITY.
DAMN STRAIGHT.

SO YOU FUCKTARDS ARE THE CREAM OF THE CROP...

... I'VE TALKED TO EACH OF YOU INDIVIDUALLY. YOU'RE THE GUYS I TRUST. YOU ALL KNOW WHAT'S AT STAKE HERE.
THE BREAKS ARE MAKING THEIR BIG MOVE. WE KNOW THIS. NOW WE'RE GONNA MAKE ONE OF OUR OWN.
THEY DON'T KNOW THEIR WEAK SPOTS --
-- BUT I DO.
THIS KEENAN WADE AND HIS PIECE OF ASS... WE'RE GONNA HIT 'EM WHERE THEY LEAST EXPECT IT.
IT'S OBVIOUS OUR FEARLESS LEADER JUST DOESN'T GET IT...

YOU THINK YOU KNOW THE SCORE OUT THERE, DREX? YOU DON'T KNOW SHIT, SCRUB.
YOUR ASS IS BENCHED. THAT MEANS YOU DON'T SOLDIER UNTIL I SAY OTHERWISE. YOU HEAR ME?!
W-WHATEVER YOU SAY, BOSS...

BULLCHUCK CAN KISS MY WHITE ASS.
WE'RE GONNA WIN THIS WAR WHETHER HE LIKES IT OR NOT.

FUNNY... I THOUGHT I'D ACTUALLY GIVEN YOU EVERYTHING YOU NEED TO GET YOUR "STORY"...
AND YET... HERE YOU ARE.
AGAIN.
NOT SO FUNNY TO ME, I CAN ASSURE YOU.
WELL, IF YOU'RE HERE TO INTERROGATE ME ABOUT ANYTHING TO DO WITH A CERTAIN SOMEONE, FORGET IT.
OTHER THAN THAT, WHAT CAN I DO FOR YOU...?

I'M NOT HERE TO TALK ABOUT HIM, ANNABELLE.
I'M HERE TO TALK ABOUT AUSTRIA. I HAVE A FEELING YOU'RE A LITTLE MORE INVOLVED THAN YOUR AVERAGE FREE-THINKING CITIZEN.

LET'S JUST SAY I HAVE A CERTAIN REPUTATION FOR PROVIDING QUALITY ENTERTAINMENT.
THE HIGHEST QUALITY, ACTUALLY. MY EMPLOYEES ARE OFTE IN HIGH DEMAND. CERTAI CLIENTS WANT WHAT THE WANT AND -- WHEN THEY PAY TOP DOLLAR -- I DO WHAT I CAN TO OBLIGE.

OCCASIONALLY, THAT INVOLVES A BIT OF TRAVEL. BUSINESS TRIPS AND WHATNOT.

I FIGURED.
ALTHOUGH I GET THE IMPRESSION THAT YOU'RE MOTIVATED BY A LOT MORE THAN MONEY.
BUT I KNOW WE'RE NOT TALKING ABOUT HIM RIGHT NOW. SO LET ME COME RIGHT OUT AND ASK...

... HAVE YOU GOT ROOM FOR ONE MORE?
YOU CAN'T BE SERIOUS.
I GO OUT OF MY WAY TO POINT YOU IN THE RIGHT DIRECTION AND NOW YOU NEED A RIDE, TOO? JULIETTE JEMAS... BIG-TIME REPORTER?!

I KNOW, I KNOW... PLEASE, THIS IS HUMILIATING ENOUGH.
BUT I THINK... I DON'T KNOW... THAT YOU WANT ME THERE.

HMMM... INTERESTING THEORY.
NOW, IF YOU'LL EXCUSE ME, I NEED TO GET BACK INSIDE.
BUSY NIGHT TONIGHT.

SIR...?
ARE YOU WAITING TO CHECK IN...?

AH, RIGHT. OKAY...
... I GUESS I NEED TO... WHAT, START SOME KIND OF TAB...?
IT'S... MY FIRST TIME...
NO PROBLEM. I CAN TAKE CARE OF YOU. WILL THIS BE CASH OR CREDIT, SIR...?
OH, CREDIT, DEFINITELY. GOT MY COMPANY CARD RIGHT HERE.
I'M SURE I CAN FIGURE OUT SOME WAY TO EXPENSE THIS, RIGHT...?

NNF!

NG!

HUHHDDT--!
PANT
PANT
PANT
DAMMIT...!

... OKAY, SO ONE OF THEIR REPS FINALLY GOT IN TOUCH AND THE TRAVEL ARRANGEMENTS HAVE BEEN NEGOTIATED.
YOU LEAVE IN EIGHT DAYS ON A PRIVATE JET ON AN AIRSTRIP OUTSIDE OF FREEMOUNT.
NOT TOO CLANDESTINE...

AND MY OFFICE JUST SENT OVER THE PAPERWORK YOU WANT LARRY TO SIGN.
I'D TRY AND TALK YOU OUT OF THAT ONE, BUT I KNOW HOW YOU ARE WHEN YOUR MIND'S MADE UP.

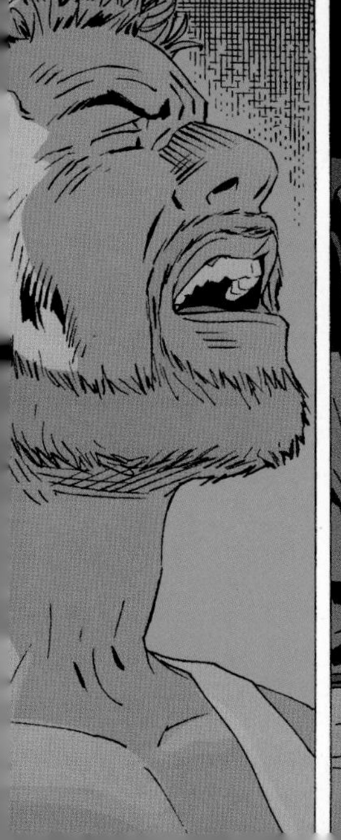

THIS LITTLE AUSTRIAN SOJOURN... YOU'RE SURE YOU DON'T WANT ME THERE? I MEAN, TRAVELLING WITH YOUR LAWYER ISN'T BEYOND THE PALE.
GOING THERE ALONE AND UNPROTECTED... WELL, IT'S AGAINST MY BETTER JUDGMENT, SIMON.

YOU THINK THIS'LL BE ANOTHER SATURNALIA? I'VE HEARD THOSE RUMORS, TOO.
THANKS BUT NO THANKS. I THINK I'LL MANAGE JUST FINE.

GUH--!

THIS IS COMPLETELY CRAZY...

... BUT IT'S NOT AS IF I'M LACKING IN AMBITION.
YOU'RE SURE YOU WANT TO DO THIS?
I ALREADY HAVE, LARRY. SO JUST TRY AND ENJOY THE ADDED PRESSURE AND THE IMPENDING ULCERS.
BESIDES, IF ALL GOES ACCORDING TO PLAN... THIS TRANSFER OF POWER IS ONLY TEMPORARY.

GOD WILLING.
I'M NOT SURE HOW MANY OF OUR CORPORATE PARTNERS ARE GOING TO ACCEPT ME AS ACTING CEO.

WELL, THAT'S THEIR PROBLEM. YOU LOOK GOOD BACK THERE.
DON'T WORRY, SIMON. I'LL KEEP YOUR SEAT WARM FOR YOU.
SURE.
YOU DO THAT.

... THINK THIS IS... JUST WHAT I NEEDED...
... GOT A... VERY STRESSFUL JOB...
DON'T EVEN SWEAT IT, "FELLOW CITIZEN"...
THAT'S RIGHT. WE'LL SAVE YOU...

... MY WIFE AT HOME... IS A NIGHTMARE...
... CAN'T... GO ON LIKE THIS...
... YOU GIRLS ARE... SO NICE...
AAAAHHHH.....

OPERATOR! CAN WE GET A RESTOCK ON THOSE PORTABLE BIO-BATTERIES...?
- DOGFIGHTS OFF BERMAN AVENUE -
... THE COUSIN DIED, SO REMY TOOK OVER THE CREW...
... HE'S GOT A NEW KIND OF WEAPON ON HIS MAIN RIDE...
HOW MUCH FOR THAT NOC LIST...?
INITIATING DIAGNOSTICS ON COLLATING.
- THE SKINS CUT A DEAL -
ALBERT EISENHOWER.
THE LIVING MIND O THE UNIVERSE PRODUCES A MYRIAD OF DAR THOUGHTS...

... I AM BUT ONE.
THE ONE AND ONLY.
YOU CAME IN SEARCH OF A NAME. YOU CAME IN SEARCH OF AN ANSWER. AN AVATAR FOR ALL HUMANITY, NO DOUBT.
VIZ IBN ZIYAD.
I AM SOMETHING MUCH MORE THAN HUMANITY COULD POSSIBLY COMPREHEND. AND YOU...

... YOU POSSESS SOMETHING I CAN USE.
YOU COME FROM THE CITY OF CONFUSION. THE POINT OF NO RETURN.
YOUR MIND IS AN ENDLESS CATALOG OF INFORMATION. THE SKELETAL INFRASTRUCTURE OF THE CITY WHICH I WILL USE TO BURN IT ALL DOWN --

-- WITH A TOUCH BY THE HAND OF GOD.

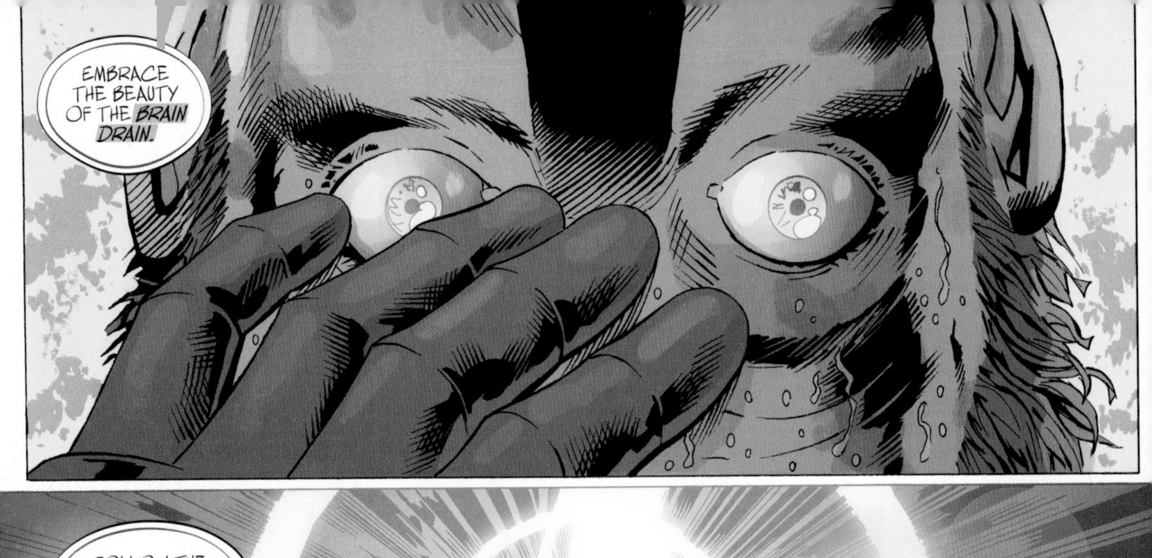
EMBRACE THE BEAUTY OF THE BRAIN DRAIN.

FOLLOW THE FIRE. LET IT BURN ALL AROUND YOU. LET IT CONSUME YOU --

-- LET IT FIND NEW PURCHASE IN A MORE APPROPRIATE VESSEL.

THERE ARE TWO WORLDS. ONE THAT HUMANITY PERCEIVES. ONE IT DOES NOT. A DUALITY THAT CANNOT BE RECONCILED BY THE HUMAN MIND.
I EXIST FAR BEYOND SUCH FRAIL LIMITATIONS. I STAND TALL WITH A FOOT FIRMLY PLANTED IN BOTH WORLDS. I SEE THE WHOLE.
ONLY ONE WHO CAN SEE THE WHOLE CAN TRULY SHAPE IT TO HIS OWN VISION.

MY EYES SEE A NEW SHAPE... AND I WILL HAVE IT.
NOW THAT YOU'VE ALL SIGNED THE VARIOUS NDAS REQUIRED FOR THIS FIELD TRIP, WE CAN BEGIN...

.. ONE THING DON'T WANT S FOR YOUR GOS TO RUN WILD JUST ECAUSE YOU ERE CHOSEN FOR THIS.
NO EMPLOYEE IS ANY MORE OR LESS VALUABLE THAN ANY OTHER. THIS WAS A RANDOM SELECTION, BASED ON SCHEDULES AND AVAILABILITY.
HAVING SAID THAT...
... YOU'RE ALL EXPECTED TO BE ON YOUR BEST BEHAVIOR. BY ALL ACCOUNTS, THESE ARE POWERFUL INDIVIDUALS YOU'LL BE SERVICING.
I KNOW WE DON'T USUALLY PERFORM HOUSE CALLS... CERTAINLY NOT THIS FAR FROM HOME. BUT THESE ARE SPECIAL CIRCUMSTANCES. JUST KEEP YOUR HEAD IN THE GAME AT ALL TIMES.
MISS LAGRAVENESE...?
I HAVE A QUESTION.
ARE THERE GOING TO BE CERTAIN... I DUNNO... EXPECTATIONS INVOLVED ON THEIR PART?
BEYOND THE USUAL, I MEAN...

THAT'S A GOOD QUESTION, TINA--
EXCUSE ME, MISS LAGRAVENESE...
ONE SECOND.

HONESTLY, I'M NOT SURE EXACTLY WHAT THESE PEOPLE ARE GOING TO BE WANTING.
ALL I CAN SUGGEST IS THAT YOU BE READY FOR ANYTHING.

... A REALLY BIG GUY IS ASKING FOR YOU. CARRYING SOMETHING... BUT I COULDN'T TELL WHAT IT WAS...
DON'T WORRY, RACHEL...
... I'LL HANDLE IT.

OKAY, WHOEVER YOU ARE... IF THIS IS MORE MESSAGING FROM THE ALPHA BROTHERS, YOU CAN FORGET IT.
NO ONE STRONG-ARMS ME IN MY OWN --
S-SORRY... I-I DIDN'T KNOW WHERE ELSE TO GO...

... CAN YOU HELP ME...?
I MEAN... HELP US?

CHAPTER THIRTY-SIX

THE DEPTHS OF HUMANITY

CHAPTER THIRTY-SIX

THE DEPTHS OF HUMANITY

THE COOKE COMPANY
... THIS IS HIGHLY UNORTHODOX. ON EVERY LEVEL.
DID HE HAPPEN TO MENTION WHEN HE'D BE *BACK?*
MAYBE WE SHOULD TAKE ANOTHER LOOK AT OUR FISCAL AGENDA--

-- MAYBE MAKE SOME *ADJUSTMENTS* CONSIDERING THE CIRCUMSTANCES...?
IT'S NOT THAT WE DON'T HAVE *CONFIDENCE,* MISS BAINES...
HE REALLY SHOULD'VE *CONSULTED* US --
SIGH ...

... OKAY, LET'S EVERYONE *SETTLE DOWN* FOR A MINUTE.
CONTRARY TO POPULAR OPINION, SIMON COOKE DOESN'T HAVE TO CLEAR *ANYTHING* WITH YOU PEOPLE.
HAVING SAID THAT, IT IS MY INTENTION FOR ALL OF US TO MOVE THIS COMPANY FORWARD *TOGETHER.*

SPEAKING OF WHICH...
... WHERE THE HELL IS *ELLIOT BARNES?*

OUR... ESTEEMED CFO HAS BEEN CONSPICUOUSLY *ABSENT* THE PAST FEW DAYS.
IT'S BECOME DAMNED *INCONVENIENT,* AS YOU CAN IMAGINE --

-- AND NO ONE KNOWS WHERE HE IS.
...
RIGHT.

I DUNNO WHAT TO TELL YA'...
... I DUNNO WHY I DID IT. BUT AFTER WHAT SHEILA DID... AND HOW SHE DID IT...
...SOMEBODY HAD TO STEP UP, Y'KNOW?

I MEAN, WHAT WOULDA HAPPENED TO HIM...?
I'M SURE I DON'T KNOW, SKYSCRAPER, BUT I HAVE A FEELING THAT BRINGING HIM HERE TO MY NIGHTCLUB JUST MIGHT GET YOU IN HOT WATER WITH SATURN SOCIAL SERVICES...

THIS KID'S STARTIN' OUT BEHIND THE EIGHT BALL. BELIEVE THAT.
IF YOU ONLY KNEW...

TO BE HONEST, I DON'T NEED TO KNOW. I DON'T WANT TO KNOW.
HE'S KIND OF A FUCKIN' MIRACLE...
WHAT WAS THAT...?
NUTHIN'.

LISTEN TO ME.
YOU MIGHT BE SUFFERING FROM SOME MOMENTARY LAPSE OF REASON. I'M SURE THIS IS ALL VERY OVERWHELMING FOR YOU...
... BUT I DON'T KNOW HOW I CAN HELP YOU HERE. THIS IS NOWHERE NEAR MY AREA OF EXPERTISE.
ALL I WANT IS TO --
WWUUAAHH!
OH SHIT.
H-HERE ... CAN YOU --
WHOA. ARE YOU CRAZY?!
DO I LOOK AT ALL MATERNAL TO YOU?! I DON'T THINK SO...!
MISS LAGRAVENESE --
-- I GOTTA TALK TO YOU!
I'M SORRY, MISS LAGRAVENESE --
-- I TRIED TO STOP HER!

I'VE GOT A PROBLEM WITH MY COMMISSION PACKAGE --
I TOLD HER TO TAKE IT UP WITH PAYROLL, MA'AM!
OH, FOR CHRIST'S SAKE...!

THOSE CREEPS IN PAYROLL CAN KISS MY --
GWAAAUUGH!
JEEZUS--!
WHERE'D THIS BABY COME FROM?!

IS THAT YOUR --
GIVE ME A BREAK, RACHEL. YOU HONESTLY THINK THAT I'D --
HOLD ON...

...WHEN IT RAINS, IT POURS.
CAN YOU PEOPLE PIPE DOWN FOR A GODDAMN SECOND?!

YES...?
MISS LAGRAVENESE...
...CAN WE SEE YOU IN THE SECURITY OFFICE?

... THIS IS... UNBELIEVABLE...
-- BUT THE GIRLS TOLD US HE STARTED MOANING ABOUT STOCK TIPS AND SHIT LIKE THAT. SO WE JUST FIGURED...
YEAH, YEAH. IT'S A DOG-EAT-DOG WORLD, FELLAS.
NORMALLY, WE DON'T MONITOR AUDIO SO CLOSELY --
WELL, WE WERE CURIOUS IF HE ACTUALLY KNEW WHAT HE WAS TALKING ABOUT...

... SO WE LOOKED HIM UP ON THE REGISTRATION FILES. TURNS OUT, HE PAID BY CREDIT CARD.
HUH. HE CERTAINLY DID --

-- THIS ONE'S A PRETTY BIG FISH.
9/25
CREDIT PURCHASE #0
SATURN CITY CENTRAL BANK
BARNES, ELLIOT K.
EXP. 11/23
COOKE COMPANY LIC
A22-8147

INTERESTING.
VERY INTERESTING.
... YOU GIRLS HAVE NO IDEA... WHERE I WORK...

... IT'S A CREW... WITHOUT A CAPTAIN...

STILL PRETTY FUCKIN' QUIET HERE...

...NO ONE COMIN' IN OR OUT.
AND NO ONE'S SHOWN UP TO RELIEVE THESE ASSHOLES --

-- I BET WE'RE GOOD AT LEAST UNTIL MORNING.
YOU'RE A GOOD SOLDIER, ALDO, SO DON'T TAKE THIS THE WRONG WAY...

...BUT YOU'RE SURE THIS IS WHERE THE ALPHA BROTHERS HANG THEIR HATS?
I MEAN, WE GOT SOME HEAVY ORDINANCE WAITIN' INSIDE.
INTEL'S AIRTIGHT ON THIS ONE, BOSS...

...UNLESS THEY KNOW WE'RE ONTO THEM. WHICH THEY MIGHT.
BUT THEY'VE GOTTEN FUCKIN' SLOPPY LATELY. THEY'RE CONFIDENT IN THEIR BIG MOVES.

THEY STILL DON'T KNOW WE'RE RUNNIN' THE SHOW NOW.
WE'RE GONNA MAKE 'EM WISH THE OLD MAN WAS STILL ALIVE AN' KICKIN'...!

HOLD UP, BOSS...
... I THINK OUR SHIT'S ABOUT TO PAY OFF BIG TIME.

HOTEL
LOOKS LIKE THE BROTHERS ARE PULLIN' IN FOR A LITTLE BREATHER –

– HELL, YES. IT'S DEFINITELY THEM.
FUCKIN' A, ALDO. CALL IN THE WAGON AND HANG BACK.
HERE WE GO, RAY. STONE COLD SOLID.

GODDAMMIT–!
WHAT'S THE PROBLEM HERE?! WE'VE GOT CREWS OUT THERE TOTALLY DROPPING THE BALL–!

WE'RE THIS CLOSE TO TAKING THE WHOLE THING AND I DON'T WANT OUR OWN GUYS FUCKING IT UP!
YOU'RE OVERREACTING, CHA CHA. AS USUAL.

DON'T GIVE ME THAT CRAP ABOUT PLAYING THE LONG GAME! THAT'S NOT HOW YOU WIN!
I WANT IT ALL -- AND I WANT IT NOW!
OKAY, OKAY. YOU KNOW THAT LEVEL OF AMBITION GETS ME ROCK HARD...
... BUT YOU'RE ABOUT TO SPIN RIGHT OFF THE PLANET--!
I CAN'T HELP IT, DOLPH... I JUST...

I KNOW, I KNOW. TAKE A DEEP BREATH.
WE'RE SO CLOSE. NOTHING'S GOING TO STOP US NOW.
THOSE TWO FUCKHEADS THINK THEY'RE UNSTOPPABLE...

... 'DIS IS GONNA BE SO SWEET.
IF IT WORKS. WE'RE TAKING A BIG CHANCE HERE, REG. SHE'S UNPREDICTABLE AS HELL.
BUT I FEEL YOU...

... TONIGHT'S THE NIGHT WE MAKE THE OLD MAN PROUD.

SO YOU'RE SUGGESTING A LITTLE ONE-ON-ONE TO TAKE THE EDGE OFF. YOU KNOW ME. I'M DOWN --
-- IF YOU ARE.

WOW.
IT'S LIKE THE AIR CHANGES WHEN YOU TWO ENTER A ROOM. THAT'S POWER RIGHT THERE.

EXACTLY THE KIND OF ACTION I'VE BEEN LOOKING FOR.

IF YOU CATCH MY DRIFT...
YOU... SHOULDN'T BE HERE.

NO? WORD ON THE STREET IS... YOU TWO ARE THE NEW KINGS OF THE NIGHTTIME WORLD.
SIDES ARE BEING DRAWN. I WANT TO BE ON THE RIGHT ONE. FIGURE THERE'S ONLY ONE WAY TO PROVE IT...

... EVEN THOUGH I DON'T USUALLY DO THIS.

This is starting to feel like a lot more than a turf war. A lot heavier than just Breaks vs. Skins.
I should know. I'm knee-deep in the shit now. Not that the Skins are much of a challenge... there's just a ton of 'em.
But I like to know what I'm fighting for. Right now I'm not so sure.
THESE IGNORANT PECKERWOODS DON'T KNOW WHE TO QUIT --
-- SO, KEENAN WADE. REPORT.
WE COUNT TWENTY SOLDIERS, PLUS A FEW AFFILIATES.
NOTHING WE COULDN'T HANDLE.
I FIGURED. YOU KNOW HOW TO CHARGE A MOTHERFUCKIN' HILL, DON'TCHA?
Masai's playing more than one game at a time. He doesn't trust anyone. Not even his own crew.

There might be a method to his madness, but he clearly wants power...

... no matter what the cost.
Y-YOU... COCK-SUCKERS--!
GOT A MOUTH ON YOU, SKIN --

-- THAT'S GOOD. MAYBE YOU'LL SAY SOME SHIT I CAN ACTUALLY USE.

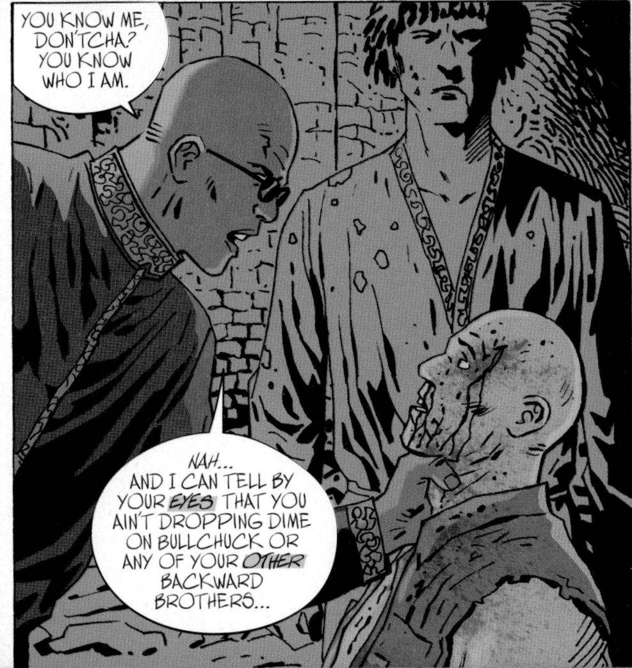
YOU KNOW ME, DON'TCHA? YOU KNOW WHO I AM.
NAH... AND I CAN TELL BY YOUR EYES THAT YOU AIN'T DROPPING DIME ON BULLCHUCK OR ANY OF YOUR OTHER BACKWARD BROTHERS...

... THAT MEANS YOU'RE ONLY GOOD FOR ONE THING.
I get it. He's not doing this for their sake...

... he's doing it for ours.
THIS IS WAR, Y'DIG?
NNNGG!

AND IN WAR, THERE'S ONLY ONE OBJECTIVE. JUST ONE.
TOTAL ANNIHILATION OF THE ENEMY.
CONSIDER YOURSELF LUCKY, WHITE BOY. YOU'VE GAZED INTO THE EYES OF GOD ~

~ NOW FUCK OFF!
--!

THAT FELT GOOD...

... BUT NOT GOOD ENOUGH.
LET HIM KNOW WE WERE HERE, TAGMAN. LET HIM KNOW I'M COMING FOR HIM.
And there it is. For Masai, it's about a lot more than just winning. This has become his holy mission. And once he's done...

BULLCHUCK-
YOU'RE NEXT!
... all of saturn city will have to bear the scars of his ambition.

FREEMOUNT:

THIS ALL FEELS... SIGNIFICANT SOMEHOW.
AND PUNCTUAL, AS WELL. A GOOD SIGN.
I THOUGHT I'D ALREADY PASSED THE INITIATION.

JUST AN OBSERVATION. I KNOW MY PEOPLE.
THEY'RE LOOKING FORWARD TO MEETING YOU. THE AGENDA FOR THIS PARTICULAR GATHERING IS QUITE COMPREHENSIVE.

I HAVE TO ADMIT... I'M GETTING MORE AND MORE CURIOUS ABOUT WHO "THEY" ARE.

EVEN IN MY LINE OF WORK, I WAS NEVER MUCH OF A HOBNOBBER. NOT AT THIS LEVEL, ESPECIALLY.
SIMON COOKE. OUTLIER TO POWER.
I THINK ALL THAT'S ABOUT TO CHANGE.

WE'LL SEE. I TEND TO HOLD *FAITH* AND *DOUBT* IN EQUAL MEASURE.
ESPECIALLY WHEN IT COMES TO POWER. WHO *HAS* IT AND WHO *WANTS* IT.

INTERESTING WAY TO FRAME IT... AS THOUGH POWER ITSELF IS SOMEHOW QUANTIFIABLE.
POWER IS *PERCEPTION.* THAT'S WHAT THE ROTHCHILD GROUP REALIZED LONG AGO.
AND PERCEPTION IS SUBJECTIVE.

NOT TO MENTION, EXTREMELY *MALLEABLE*. ALL IT TAKES IS THE *WILL* TO CHANGE THINGS.
I MAKE NO PROMISES, MISTER WEBER. THEN AGAIN, I'M *HERE*... SO THAT SHOULD TELL YOU *SOMETHING*...
IT DOES, ABSOLUTELY. BUT I KNEW A LONG TIME AGO YOU WERE ONE OF US.
DESPITE YOUR INHERENT *ISOLATIONISM*, I THINK YOU'LL BE *SURPRISED* HOW MUCH WE HAVE IN COMMON...
...AND HOW MUCH WE CAN ACCOMPLISH TOGETHER.
KUMBAYA.

NOT QUITE SO HARMONIOUS, I'LL GIVE YOU THAT.
BUT THE GREATEST VICTORIES ARE OFTEN THE HARDEST WON. SURELY THAT'S OBVIOUS.

WE SHOULDN'T GET AHEAD OF OURSELVES. ALL WILL BE REVEALED SOON ENOUGH.
FOR NOW... AUSTRIA AWAITS.

RIGHT.
I'M SURE SATURN CITY CAN SURVIVE FOR A WHILE WITHOUT ME.

IT HAS NOW BEGUN. ONCE AGAIN, A VISION.
A NEW LENS THROUGH WHICH ALL OF REALITY WILL BE FOCUSED.
DEADLY WHEELS IN MOTION...

... ITS OWN MOMENTUM, A TERRIFYING CERTAINTY.

MESSENGERS OF DARKNESS, ARMED WITH NEW PURPOSE.

YOU WILL RAIN FIRE DOWN UPON THEM. THEY WILL KNOW THEIR MAKER IS ANGERED.
AND NOW... THE MAKER WILL REMAKE WHAT HE ALONE HAS CONSTRUCTED.

THE CONSCIOUS MIND...

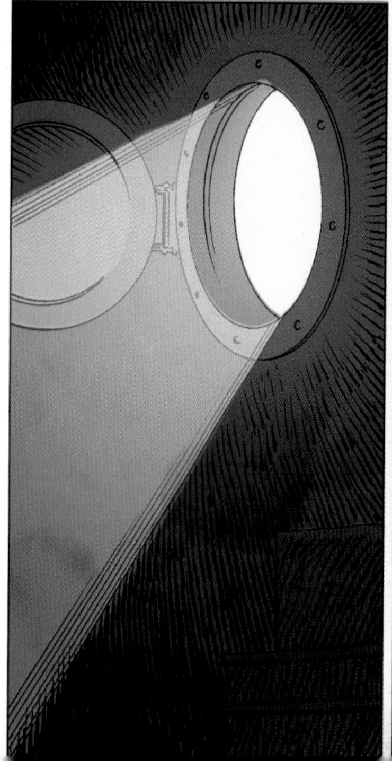

...AND THE LIZARD BRAIN.

YOUR FINAL RECKONING IS NOW.

THIS IS IT--

-- REMEMBER, WE'RE GOING IN HARD AND FAST.
ONE THING, DREXLER... ARE WE SIGNING OUR WORK OR WHAT?
YOU MEAN, DO WE WANT 'EM TO KNOW IT WAS THE SKINS WHO DID THIS?

OH, HELL YES.

C'MON, C'MON, C'MON...!
YOU BETTER ANSWER YOUR PHONE, GODDAMMIT...!

WHA--?
S-SOMEBODY OUT THERE...?!
KEENAN...?

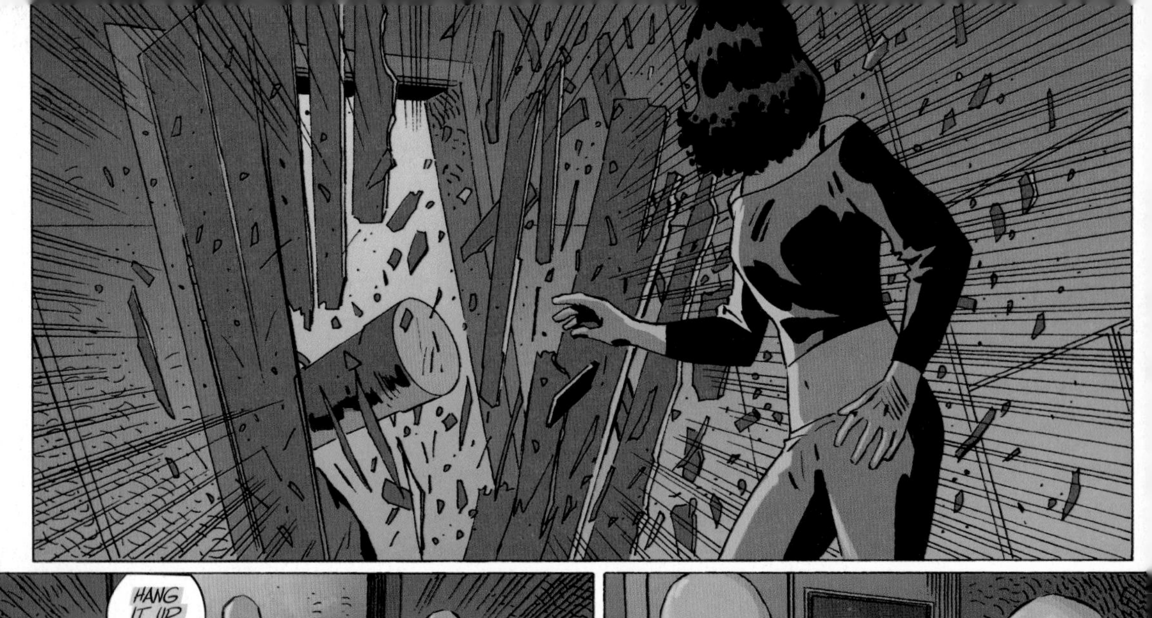

HANG IT UP BITCH!
FIND THAT BREAK COCK-SUCKER--!
WHAT THE FUCK--?!

YOU CRACKERS GOTTA BE OUTTA YOUR FUCKIN' MINDS--!
H-HEY! LEGGO!
WHO DO YOU THINK YOU ARE--

-- BARKING AT MY CREW LIKE THAT?!
YOU GOT A HOLE ON YOU, DONTCHA? AND AN ATTITUDE TO MATCH.
NOW... AT SOME POINT YOU MAY START WONDERING HOW YOU GOT CAUGHT UP IN ALL THIS...
... BUT YOU ALREADY KNOW HOW.

YOU PICKED THE WRONG DICK TO SUCK, SISTER...
... AND NOW YOU'RE GONNA PAY FOR IT.

CHAPTER THIRTY-SEVEN

SATURN'S BRILLIANT PARADE

CHAPTER THIRTY-SEVEN

SATURN'S BRILLIANT PARADE

YOU THINK WE DON'T KNOW WHO YOU ARE... OR WHAT YOU'RE ALL ABOUT...?
YOU'RE NOT THE ONLY ONE HERE WITH A REP...
THE REAL QUESTION IS...
... DO YOU THINK YOU CAN HANDLE BOTH OF US...?
I THINK I KNOW SOMETHING ABOUT THE ALPHA BROTHERS...
... BUT I HAVE A FEELING THERE'S A LOT MORE TO UNCOVER.
S-SO... THE CURIOUS TYPE...
INTENSELY CURIOUS.
I'VE GOT AN ITCH...
... YOU THINK YOU COULD GIVE IT A LITTLE SCRATCH...?

Y'KNOW, I'M ALL ABOUT THE FEELS...
...I CAN FIND WHAT'S DEEP INSIDE...
WHAT'RE YOU --
JUST LET IT HAPPEN, BABY...

... THERE'S A COUPLE OF HARD MEN IN THERE...
S-SOME-THING'S... NOT RIGHT...
DON'T RESIST IT...
... SURRENDER TO IT...
... IT'S GOING TO BE SO GOOD...!

ELLIOT!
YOU ASSHOLE --
-- WHAT IS GOING THROUGH THAT THICK HEAD OF YOURS?!
DO YOU KNOW YOUR OFFICE HAS BEEN CALLING NONSTOP LOOKING FOR YOU?!
WHAT KIND OF DEADBEAT GAME ARE YOU PLAYING?!
ANSWER ME, YOU PATHETIC LOSER!
...
YOU CERTAINLY WOULDN'T UNDER-STAND...!
DON'T YOU DARE TAKE THAT TONE WITH ME!
YOU THINK YOU'RE ABLE TO JUST DO WHATEVER YOU WANT-- WHENEVER YOU WANT?!
YOU KNOW BETTER THA THAT --

YYAAHH!!
UHHH... GWHUH~!

BITCH~!
DON'T TOUCH ME AGAIN!
I'LL KILL YOU~!

WORTHLESS PIECE OF SHIT ~
GGYYUUHH~!

GODDAMMIT!

THAT'S IT!
FINALLY TIME TO TEACH YOU A LESSON!
I'M SICK OF YOU TREATING ME LIKE I'M NOTHING!

I'LL SHOW YOU HOW "NOTHING" I AM!
I'M THE MAN NOW!

IT'S TIME TO FACE FACTS. WITH MISTER COOKE CURRENTLY... INDISPOSED, CERTAIN FINANCIAL ISSUES HAVE UNFORTUNATELY COME TO LIGHT.
AND A MISSING CFO DOESN'T HELP, EITHER...!
WELL, THAT GOES WITHOUT SAYING...
... BUT THESE ISSUES NEED TO BE ADDRESSED, MISS BAINES. AND THE SOONER, THE BETTER.
MISTER COOKE LEFT YOU IN CHARGE, BUT HE MAY HAVE FAILED TO INFORM YOU OF CERTAIN PRE-EXISTING CONDITIONS...
IT'S BECOME CLEAR THAT THERE ARE SEVERAL REVENUE STREAMS THAT AREN'T FLOWING AS THEY SHOULD...
IF ANYTHING THIS IS AN OPPORTUNITY
HOLD ON. WHAT EXACTLY ARE YOU FOLKS IMPLYING...?
MISTER COOKE HAD SET UP A SYSTEM WHERE CERTAIN DEPARTMENTS WERE INTER-DEPENDENT ON EACH OTHER.
FINANCIALLY SPEAKING, THAT IS.
ELLIOT BARNES WAS A MASTER OF CROSS COLLATERALIZATION
IN ANY CASE, THERE ARE AREAS WHERE WE'RE JUST LEAVING MONEY ON THE TABLE...
THE R&D DEPARTMENT, FOR EXAMPLE --
SIGH
OKAY, LET'S JUST PAY THE A LITTLE VISIT.
AS YOU'RE WELL AWARE, IT'S PROBABLY THE MOST SECRETIVE OUT OF ALL OF COOKE'S DEPARTMENTS...!
WE'VE HEARD RUMORS OF SERIOUS INQUIRIES REGARDING THE SPECIFIC WORK THEY'RE DOING...
A LOT OF IT, EVEN WE DON'T HAVE ACCESS TO...!

SHOULD WE HAVE BEEN... I DON'T KNOW... STERILIZED BEFORE WE CAME IN HERE? PUT ON SOME SORT OF PROTECTIVE GEAR, MAYBE...?
DON'T BE PARANOID, KELVIN...!
I JUST WANT AN OVERVIEW STRAIGHT FROM THE SUPERVISOR'S MOUTH...
MISS BAINES! HAVE THE PENTAGON LIAISONS BEEN IN TOUCH? WE KEEP SENDING THEM YOUR WAY...
DID YOU RECEIVE OUR SUMMARY ON NEW POLYMER STRENGTHS THAT WE PUT TOGETHER?
WAIT A MINUTE. ONE AT A TIME --
ANY CHANCE YOU'RE HERE TO REVIEW OUR NEWEST STEALTH HULL SAMPLES...?
WE'RE HOPING THIS CHANGE OF LEADERSHIP RESULTS IN A RENEWED COMMITMENT TO THE WORK WE DO HERE --
MISTER COOKE ALWAYS KEPT US IN THE DARK --
-- CORPORATE NDAS ARE TOO RESTRICTIVE --
-- SURELY YOU'RE IN A POSITION TO EXPLOIT OUR POTENTIAL --
... TOMORROW YOU HAVE AN EXTREMELY FULL SCHEDULE, MISS BAINES.
HUMAN RESOURCES AT NINE. THEN A FOLLOW-UP MEETING ON DIVISIONAL STRUCTURE METHODS.
FASCINATING. ANYTHING ELSE...?
QUITE A BIT, MA'AM. THE TECH DIVISION NEEDS YOUR APPROVAL ON THEIR NEW DEMO SEQUENCE.
THEN LUNCH WITH MID-LEVEL DEPARTMENT HEADS CONCERNING THE COST BREAKDOWN IN YOUR INBOX. THEN A CONFERENCE CALL WITH THE SATURN ZONING COMMISSION...

THE AUSTRIAN ALPS:
WELCOME TO THE INTERALPEN HOTEL TYROL...

...AS YOU CAN SEE, THINGS ARE RAMPING UP. MEMBERS ARRIVING FROM EVERY CORNER OF THE CIVILIZED WORLD.
JUST DON'T BE SURPRISED AT SOME OF THE FACES YOU SEE IN ATTENDANCE. IT'LL ALL MAKE SENSE EVENTUALLY, I ASSURE YOU.

IS IT ALWAYS THIS BUSY...?
THINGS WILL CALM DOWN CONSIDERABLY ONCE EVERYONE IS SETTLED IN.

THINK OF THIS PLACE AS SANCTUARY, SIMON. A PLACE TO ACHIEVE A RENEWED SENSE OF MUCH-NEEDED GLOBAL PERSPECTIVE.
BUT, YES, THERE'S ALWAYS A BIT OF NERVOUS ENERGY FLYING AROUND AT THE BEGINNING OF THESE THINGS. EVERYONE FINDS THEIR FOCUS SOON ENOUGH.
SPEAKING OF WHICH, WE ARRANGED FOR CERTAIN CREATURE COMFORTS THAT YOU MIGHT FIND HELPFUL IN THAT REGARD.

AFTER ALL, WE DON'T WANT YOU GETTING HOMESICK ON US.
NOW, LET'S GET YOU CHECKED IN TO YOUR ROOM...

THIS JOB MAY PAY OFF SIX MONTHS' WORTH OF RENT...

... I JUST HOPE IT DOESN'T COST ME IN, I DUNNO, OTHER WAYS...
LIKE YOUR SOUL? DON'T BE PARANOID, SUZI. WE'VE ALL HEARD THE RUMORS.
WELL, I KNOW WE'RE NOT SUPPOSED TO TALK ABOUT IT, BUT IF ANY OF THEM ARE TRUE, THEN I'M A LITTLE FREAKED...

IT'S ALL ABOUT THE ENJAMINS, ALI. T SPEAKING OF FREAKY SHIT...
... ANYONE KNOW HER...?

SHE'S NOT FROM THE CLUB, IS SHE?
DID MISS LAGRAVENESE BRING IN A RINGER? OR MAYBE A SPECIAL REQUEST...?
DOES IT MATTER? IT'S PRETTY OBVIOUS...

... SHE'S NOT ONE OF US.

SIMON COOKE...

... I SEE YOU'VE ARRIVED AND THAT YOU'VE MADE YOURSELF COMFORTABLE. I'M CERTAINLY RELIEVED THAT YOU'VE MADE IT THIS FAR.
PLEASE ALLOW ME TO INTRODUCE MYSELF.
MY NAME IS LIGETI.

WELL, CONSIDERING THAT NAME DOESN'T RING ANY *BELLS* MEANS YOU PROBABLY HOLD A FAIRLY HIGH RANK...
I'VE NEVER BEEN THE TYPE TO PROMOTE NOTORIETY.
AS YOU CAN IMAGINE, IT'S EXTREMELY BAD FOR BUSINESS.
DEPENDS ON THE *BUSINESS*, I SUPPOSE.

VERY TRUE. BUT I'M NOT HERE TO BE GLIB.
THERE'S BEEN A FAIR AMOUNT OF DISCUSSION WHEN IT COMES TO YOUR PRESENCE HERE. I WOULDN'T GO SO FAR AS TO USE THE WORD, "PROBATIONARY," HOWEVER --
MISTER LIGETI...

... YOU'RE NOT THE *ONLY* ONE WITH CONCERNS. BELIEVE ME.
BUT YOUR OWN *MISTER WEBER* WENT TO GREAT LENGTHS TO GET ME HERE.
I'VE ARRIVED WITH AN *OPEN MIND*. I DON'T KNOW IF THAT MATTERS TO *YOU*, THOUGH...

IT MATTERS, MISTER COOKE.
I GUESS WE'LL BOTH DISCOVER TO WHAT EXTENT IN TIME.

... AND HE HAD THE NERVE TO CALL HIMSELF A *DIPLOMAT*...!
... WELL, HE'S ALL ABOUT FINDING THE LEGAL LOOPHOLES, RIGHT?
BY THE WAY, YOUR ENGLISH IS REALLY *IMPROVING*, AMBASSADOR...

... PERHAPS THIS YEAR WE WILL FINALLY GET INTO TRADE DISCUSSIONS...
DON'T HOLD YOUR BREATH, DIMITRI.
BESIDES, YOU KNOW WE BEGIN WITH PHILOSOPHY AND RITUAL...

I'M MORE INTERESTED IN MOVEMENT...
... WHAT GOOD IS POWER AND INFLUENCE IF WE DON'T USE THEM?

MISTER COOKE...?
FORGIVE ME, BUT I AM YOUR PERSONAL ATTENDANT ASSIGNED TO YOU FOR THE DURATION OF YOUR STAY HERE.
AHHH... YES. THEY SAID YOU'D FIND ME. AND YOUR NAME IS...?

NO NAMES, MISTER COOKE. IT'S NOT NECESSARY FOR OUR RELATIONSHIP.
THERE ARE MUCH MORE IMPORTANT RELATIONSHIPS FOR YOU TO CULTIVATE. IN THE MEANTIME...

...I'M HERE TO SEE TO YOUR EVERY NEED.
...
RIG

NOW THERE'S CONFLICT!
DERRUBÁ-LO!
SHOW HIM WHAT FOR, YEAH!

VOGLIO VEDERE IL SANGUE!
NO JUDGMENTS!
DO IT!

I DON'T KNOW IF THESE ARE SETUPS OR NOT!
BUT WHO CARES?!
TAKE HIM DOWN!

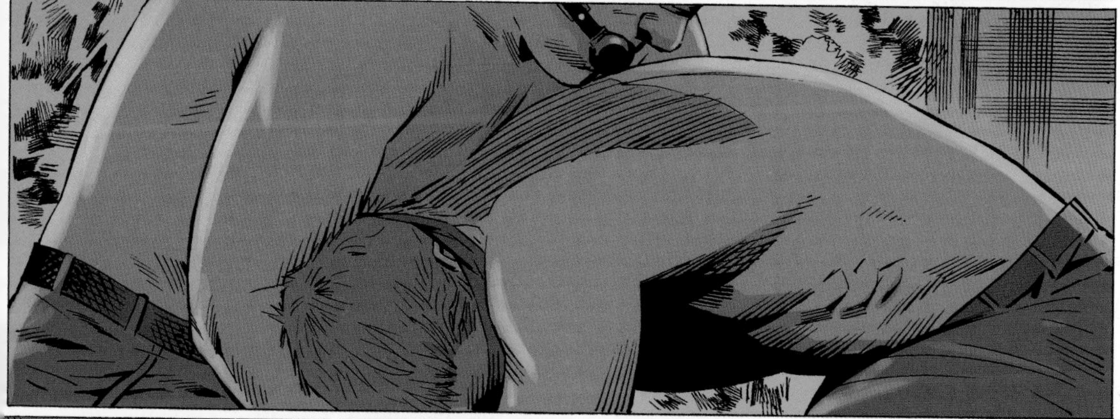

AHHH... DON'T LOOK NOW, CEDRIC...
... BUT IT APPEARS WE HAVE AN AUDIENCE.
MMM...?

APOLOGIES... BUT WE ARE IN A FLOW.
UNLESS YOU'D CARE TO JOIN IN. ALTHOUGH I SEE BY YOUR EXPRESSION THAT YOU'D RATHER NOT.

BE MINDFUL, DEAR BOY --

-- IT'S NOT WHAT YOU SEE HERE THAT MATTERS...
... IT'S WHAT YOU DO HERE.

MISTER COOKE.
FORGIVE ME, BUT TODAY IS THE FIRST FULL DAY OF SCHEDULED EVENTS, AND YOU MUST PREPARE.
I ASSUME YOU'VE BEEN BRIEFED ON TODAY'S AGENDA. ATTENDANCE IS MANDATORY.

ALL PARTICIPANTS ARE REQUIRED TO WEAR INDIVIDUALIZED, CEREMONIAL HEAD GEAR.
IT IS NOT A MATTER OF ANONYMITY...
... IT IS MERELY TRADITION.

ATTENTION, ONE AND ALL. LET US BEGIN AGAIN.
WITH THIS NOBLE AND PRESTIGIOUS GATHERING, WE COLLECTIVELY SURRENDER TO THE NEW AGE OF EMPOWERMENT.
EVEN THOSE WITH VIRGIN MINDS HAVE SEEN THE NEED...
... THE DAYS OF IDLE HANDS AND EMPTY HOPE ARE LONG GONE. FINALLY, ALL PRETENSE HAS BEEN ABANDONED.
WE ARE ALL WEAVING SPIDERS HERE.

THIS IS NO TEDDY BEAR PICNIC. WE COME HERE TO FIND PURPOSE, DO WE NOT?
THE WORLD SPINS UNWAVERINGLY UPON ITS AXIS. WE FEEL IT BENEATH OUR FEET. A CONSTANT OF NATURE REGARDLESS OF THE WHIMS OF MAN.
BUT PROGRESS IS ONLY ACHIEVABLE THROUGH PRECISE ACTION.
THAT'S WHAT WE'VE ALL COME HERE FOR.

MASTERS OF FINANCE. OF INDUSTRY. OF POLITICS. OF OPINION.
THE STEERING COMMITTEE HAS VETTED YOU ALL... AND SO WE ARE ABLE TO COME HERE AND SPEAK FRANKLY.

PRETTY MUCH THE SAME SPEECH EVERY YEAR. A FEW REFINEMENTS HERE AND THERE.
A LOT OF THIS IS JUST CEREMONY...

...WE'LL GET DOWN TO BUSINESS SOON ENOUGH.

...BORDERS DO NOT SEPARATE US. NOR DOES RACE. OR BLOODLINE.
HISTORY WILL ULTIMATELY SHOW WHAT WE SET INTO MOTION HERE...

...AS IT ALWAYS HAS.

SATURN CITY:
THE THIRTEENTH FLOOR:
CREEPY IN HERE, RIGHT...?
WHO THE HELL--?!
RELAX. I'M A FRIEND OF SIMON'S.
MOSTLY.
YOU WANT TO BE MORE SPECIFIC...?
ANNABELLE LAGRAVENESE. I'M... A LOCAL BUSINESS OWNER.
I DIDN'T EXPECT ANYONE WOULD ACTUALLY BE HERE.
SO... IN THE SPIRIT OF TIT-FOR-TAT... WHO MIGHT YOU BE?

LORRAINE BAINES. LARRY, ACTUALLY. ACTING CEO FOR THE COOKE COMPANY.
I'M ASSUMING THAT YOU'RE HERE BECAUSE YOU'RE FAMILIAR WITH SIMON'S... PAST.
TO SAY THE LEAST.

WELL, I HAVEN'T BEEN ON THE INSIDE THAT LONG. I IMAGINE THAT YOU...
LET'S JUST SAY I'VE KNOWN FOR A WHILE. HE AND I... WE HAVE A CERTAIN UNDERSTANDING.
SO HOW'S THE JOB GOING? SIMON NEVER SEEMED TO GROK TO IT WITH ANY GENUINE ENTHUSIASM...

A SOURCE OF SOME FRUSTRATION AT THE TIME, TRUST ME. BUT I HAD NO IDEA...!
AT LEAST HE HAD A REASON. A FOCUS. NOW THAT'S GONE... EVEN THOUGH HE'S ONTO SOMETHING ELSE NOW...

WELL, I'M NOT HERE TO DISCUSS THE ILLUMINATI.
AND AS MUCH AS I DON'T WANT TO INTERRUPT HIS CRUSADE, I'VE GOT SOME INFO THAT I THINK HE SHOULD KNOW.
I WAS GOING TO USE THE GEAR IN HERE TO SEND HIM AN ENCRYPTED MESSAGE. FIGURED THAT WAS THE SAFEST WAY.

MAYBE SO. HONESTLY, I DON'T KNOW HOW THESE GADGETS WORK. SOME OF THE TECHNOLOGY IS JUST... I DUNNO...
IS THIS INFO OF A PERSONAL NATURE...?
I SUPPOSE IT DEPENDS...
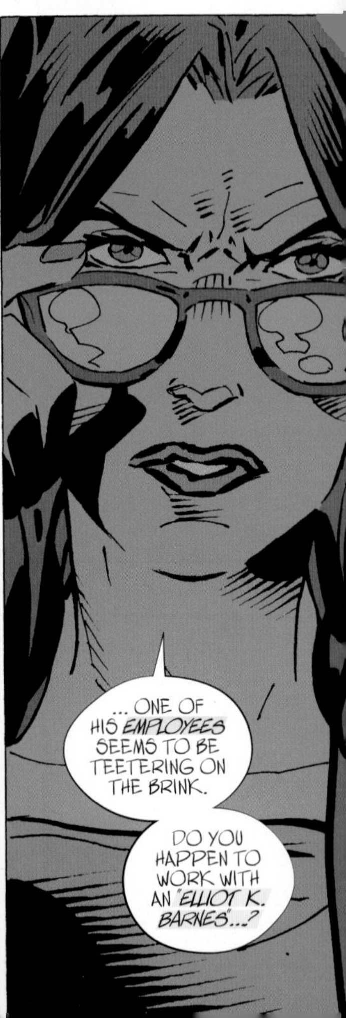
... ONE OF HIS EMPLOYEES SEEMS TO BE TEETERING ON THE BRINK.
DO YOU HAPPEN TO WORK WITH AN "ELLIOT K. BARNES"...?

CHAPTER THIRTY-EIGHT

THE REPTILIAN ELITE

CHAPTER THIRTY-EIGHT

THE REPTILIAN ELITE

It's been a few days now. You still haven't opened your eyes, Vernita.
And I'm sitting here, trying to figure out how things got so fucked up.
You're still so beautiful.
And I'm just... filled up with ugliness...

... the deepest darkness...
... the horror of knowing right away what had happened...
... and what they did to you.

I know you tried to warn me. You were worried I was in over my head. I said I knew what I was doing.
But I never once thought to consider my greatest vulnerability...
... you.

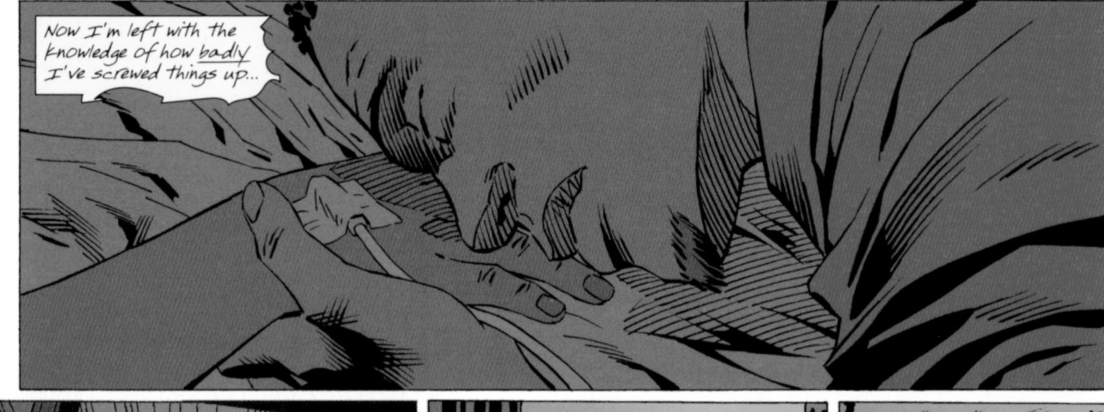
Now I'm left with the knowledge of how badly I've screwed things up...

... and the memory of finding you there. On the floor. Beaten and broken.
This war... the Breaks and the skins... it's all bullshit. I know that now.
This kind of collateral damage gives me a new perspective.
There's only one way out of this now...

... and that's to take it all the way.

UHH!
PANT!
PANT!
GUH--!

NNUHHH--!
PANT!
PANT!

... IT WAS ALL GOING ACCORDING TO PLAN. NO FUSS, NO MUSS.
I WASN'T EXPECTING ANY REAL SURPRISES HERE...

... THEN AGAIN, I WAS GOING IN COLD --
DON'T GIMME NO BULLSHIT INTEL ARGUMENT --

-- WHAT THE FUCK IS GOING ON IN THERE?!
I'M NOT ARGUING. I'M EXPLAINING...

... THERE'S A CHANCE WE DIDN'T KNOW EVERYTHING THERE IS TO KNOW ABOUT THESE TWO --
DID YOU GET 'EM OR WHAT?!

I DID. SORT OF.
THESE TWO ARE A LOT MORE SYMBIOTIC THAN YOU REALIZE. THEY FEED OFF EACH OTHER. THEY CAN GIVE EACH OTHER STRENGTH.
THE FUCK ARE YOU TALKIN' ABOUT?!

I HAD THEM BOTH. AT LEAST, I THOUGHT I DID. AND THEN... WELL...
... ONE OF THEM BASICALLY SACRIFICED HIMSELF SO THE OTHER COULD MAKE A BREAK FOR IT. BUT DON'T WORRY...

... I THINK I GOT THE BEST ONE.

GEPÄCKAUS
BAGGAGE CLAIM
G B.C.D.
AUSGANG / EXIT
ANYONE ELSE FREEZING THEIR NIPPLES OFF...?!
WE GOTTA GO OUT IN THIS MESS, I'M ASKING FOR A BONUS...
AUSTRIA:

... I MEAN, I DIDN'T EXACTLY BRING THE WARDROBE TO DEAL WITH --
LADIES...

... MAY I PLEASE HAVE YOUR ATTENTION?
DUE TO THE INCLEMENT WEATHER, WE'LL BE TAKING YOU TO YOUR FINAL DESTINATION VIA THE SNOWCATS THAT ARE ARRIVING AS WE SPEAK.

NOW I'M SURE I DON'T HAVE TO TELL YOU THAT WHAT YOU WITNESS FROM THIS POINT ON IS HIGHLY CONFIDENTIAL.
WE EXPECT YOU TO LOOK AND ACT PROFESSIONAL.
Y-YES SIR.

EXCELLENT. OKAY, THE FIRST RIDE IS PULLING UP NOW.
LET'S GET YOU ALL LOADED UP AND GET THIS SHOW ON THE ROAD...

THE RITUAL CAN NOW BEGIN...

... SINCE WE HAVE ALL GATHERED TOGETHER, LET US REAFFIRM OUR BELIEFS IN THE MANNER PRACTICED BY THE ANCIENTS ACROSS THE AGES.
WITHIN THE *EFFIGY* THAT LOOMS OVER US, THERE IS *POWER.* THERE IS *PURPOSE.* WITHIN ITS *SHADOW,* MANKIND RESIDES... IGNORANT OF HIS OWN DESTINY. SUBJUGATED BY THE WAYS OF THE NATURAL WORLD AND THE POWER IT SEEMS TO POSSESS.
BUT WE KNOW THE TRUTH. WE KNOW HOW *REAL* POWER IS ACHIEVED.
IT IS RIGHT HERE AMONG US....
... WITHIN *US.*

WE HAVE COME HERE TO *DEFY* THE DIVINE WILL OF X'ULTA.
X'ULTA NO LONGER CONTROLS OUR DESTINY.

AND HOW DO WE DEMONSTRATE OUR INDEPENDENCE...?
WE BRING FORTH THE ELEMENT THAT MOST REPRESENTS MANKIND'S DOMINANCE OVER THE SPIRITUAL SHADOWS OF EVIL...
... WE BRING FIRE.
WE GATHER HERE AS THE WORLD'S ELITE. TOGETHER WE WILL UNITE OUR WORLD, ONCE AND FOR ALL.
THERE WILL BE CHAOS. THERE WILL BE DISORDER. BUT OUT OF THESE THINGS WILL COME A REVELATION...
... WE ALL KNOW THIS TO BE SO.

TOO MANY OF OUR FELLOW MEN HAVE SUCCUMBED TO X'ULTA'S INFLUENCE. THE GREAT UNWASHED HAVE SUFFERED FROM THEIR BLINDNESS FOR FAR TOO LONG.
BUT OUR CONTROL IS STRONG. OUR CONTROL IS VAST. AND SO WE TAKE OUR FIRE --
-- AND USE IT TO LIGHT THE WAY FORWARD.
WATCH IT BURN, FELLOW CHILDREN...
... BATHE IN ITS RIGHTEOUS WARMTH.
ALLOW ITS GLOW TO ILLUMINATE YOU.
TOGETHER, LET US VOICE OUR SUPREMACY OVER A DYING SYSTEM, ONE AND ALL...

ONE WORLD, ONE MIND, ONE HOPE... FROM X'ULTA'S ASHES WE RISE...
KEEP IT UP! LET THIS CHANT REVERBERATE THROUGHOUT ALL OF HISTORY ~
-- WITH EACH AND EVERY CEREMONY, WE TAKE ONE STEP CLOSER TO A WORLD THAT FINALLY MAKES SENSE...
... A WORLD WHERE WE CAN FINALLY TRANSCEND THE EVILS OF MAN.
THIS WORLD IS OURS.
HALLELUJAH.

YOU ARE READY...
... YOU HAVE BEEN GIVEN ALL THAT YOU WILL EVER NEED.
GIVEN BY ME.
NO MORE QUESTIONS. NO MORE UNCERTAINTY. YOUR MISSION IS ALL THAT IS....

... YOU ARE CHARGED WITH UNLEASHING MY ETERNAL WRATH.
LET IT SPREAD ACROSS THE SCARRED FACE OF THE NEW CITY.

UNDERSTAND HE ATTENDED THE CREMATION CEREMONY.
I WONDER IF HE TOOK IT IN THE SPIRIT IT WAS INTENDED...
AND WHAT SPIRIT IS *THAT*, MISTER WEBER...?

DON'T GET ME WRONG. OBVIOUSLY I RESPECT THE TRADITIONS.
BUT I BROUGHT HIM HERE FOR A SPECIFIC *REASON*.

HAVE YOU HAD ANY PERSONAL CONTACT WITH --
I'VE *SPOKEN* TO YOUR DISTINGUISHED MISTER COOKE AND I'M STILL... *UNDECIDED*.

MY FIRST IMPRESSION IS THAT SIMON COOKE IS A *LOST SOUL*... STRUGGLING WITH HIS OWN SELF-ACTUALIZATION.
I GET THE SENSE THAT *HE* IS, TOO.
WELL... THAT'S POSSIBLE...
NOT EXACTLY PRIME ROTHCHILD MATERIAL...

I WOULD HAVE TO *DISAGREE* WITH THAT ASSESSMENT, SIR.
HE'LL CATCH ON ONCE HE INTERACTS WITH SOME OF THE OTHER MEMBERS.

THAT REMAINS TO BE SEEN. THERE ARE DELICATE ISSUES BEING ADDRESSED THIS YEAR. WE CANNOT ABIDE A SPOILER OF ANY KIND.
IF HIS PRESENCE HERE PROVES TO BE AN OBSTRUCTION TO OUR PROGRESS, THERE WILL BE DIRE CONSEQUENCES. FOR *HIM*...

...AND FOR *YOU*.

WELL, THAT WAS... INVIGORATING AS ALWAYS...!
I'M STILL BAFFLED HOW GOOD OL' X'ULTA SHOWS UP AT EVERY MEETING, NO MATTER WHERE IN THE WORLD WE HOLD IT...
MOVIE MAGIC, PROBABLY.

... BUT THERE WILL BE MAGIC MADE HERE. OF THAT, YOU CAN BE CERTAIN.
AS LONG AS WE'RE THE MAGICIANS. THEREIN LIES THE TRICK.
MISTER COOKE, IS IT? MY NAME IS FRANCIS.
A PLEASURE.
I ASSUME YOU'RE USING THE TERM "MAGIC" LOOSELY...
JUST ABOUT EVERY TERM IS SUBJECTIVE IN THIS ENVIRONMENT...

...
WAIT A MINUTE. AREN'T YOU SUPPOSED TO BE --
DON'T BELIEVE EVERYTHING YOU READ, SON. AS IT HAPPENS, MY PUBLIC PERSONA WAS BECOMING SOCIALLY INCONVENIENT.
RIGHT.
I LEARNED LONG AGO THAT REAL POWER HAS LITTLE TO DO WITH THE TITLE YOU HOLD.
MOST ELECTED OFFICIALS ARE BLISSFULLY IGNORANT OF HOW THE WORLD WORKS. WHAT THEY EXCEL AT... IS BUYING INTO THE BIG LIE.

THE BIG LIE, HUH? GLAD I DIDN'T VOTE FOR YOU.
HA... THAT'S FUNNY. AS IF VOTING ACTUALLY MATTERS.
IT'S ALL POMP AND CIRCUMSTANCE. A BIG ENTERTAINMENT. LISTEN CAREFULLY, YOU CAN HEAR THE SOUNDTRACK.
WE SPEND MOST OF OUR TIME LISTENING. THE REST OF THE TIME... WE ACT.
THE DECISIONS WE MAKE... THE ACTIONS WE TAKE... THEY MAKE THE WORLD TURN.

I'M SURE YOU HAVE SOME INKLING OF --
OIL PRICES IN THE SEVENTIES. THE BRODY PLAN. THATCHER'S OUSTING. TORONTO HYDRO.
AND THOSE JUST SCRATCH THE SURFACE.

HE'S GOOD...!
SO IT SEEMS. NICE TO KNOW THE STEERING COMMITTEE STILL HAS AN EYE FOR TALENT.
BE CAREFUL, THOUGH...

.. TALENT IS ONE THING. VISION IS QUITE ANOTHER.
I'M SURE WE'LL SPEAK AGAIN... ON THE INSIDE.

FORGIVE THE INTRUSION, MISTER COOKE...

... BUT I AM CHARGED WITH ESCORTING YOU SAFELY BACK TO THE HOTEL.
THERE ARE SEVERAL *MEETINGS* YOU SHOULD ATTEND BEFORE THEY BREAK FOR THE EVENING.
AS A GUEST, YOU SEEM TO BE IN HIGH DEMAND...
OH YEAH... I'M THE BELLE OF THE BALL, ALRIGHT. THEY CAN'T GET *ENOUGH* OF ME.

THERE'S... A LOT OF *THEATRE* INVOLVED, ISN'T THERE?
DUE RESPECT, MISTER COOKE...

... BUT IT'S NOT MY PLACE TO COMMENT ON SUCH THINGS.
HOWEVER... IDENTITY OBFUSCATION MAY OFTEN SEEM *NECESSARY*... IN ORDER TO ACHIEVE CERTAIN *GOALS*.
NOW... IF YOU WOULD BE SO KIND AS TO RESTORE YOUR *MASK* ONCE AGAIN...

SURE.
Y'KNOW, IF YOU KNEW THE SHEER AMOUNT OF *IRONY* AT WORK WHE IT COMES TO *ME* WEARING THIS THING...

... IT WOULD BREAK YOUR FUCKING BRAIN.

CITY HALL:
YOU PEOPLE DON'T SEEM TO GRASP THE OBVIOUS ~

-- THIS WHOLE THING IS SPINNING OUT OF CONTROL! ANYONE CARE TO TELL ME WHY?!
MAYOR SEDGWICK, WE'RE GETTING SIMILAR REPORTS FROM EVERY PRECINCT ON THE ISLAND.
THEY'RE OVERWHELMED AND UNDERSTAFFED. THE GANGS HAVE THEM OUTNUMBERED THREE TO ONE.

THIS TURF WAR IS --
I'M SICK OF HEARING ABOUT HOW OUR OWN POLICE FORCE CAN'T HANDLE THINGS WHEN THE SHIT HITS THE FAN!
I REFUSE TO SIT BACK AND WATCH THIS CITY BURN ITSELF TO THE GODDAMN GROUND!
I WANT SOLUTIONS! I WANT ACTION! UNTIL THEN ~
-- GET THE FUCK OUT!

LOOKS LIKE I'M NOT THE ONLY ONE HAVING A TOUGH DAY AT THE OFFICE...
... HOPE IT ISN'T ANYTHING SERIOUS.
I ALSO HOPE YOU DON'T MIND... I LET MYSELF IN.

WELL, WELL, WELL... IF IT ISN'T MISS COOKE COMPANY HERSELF...
... HOW'S LIFE BEHIND THE BIG DESK?
NOT EVERY-THING IT'S CRACKED UP TO BE, TRUST ME.
SIMON'S OUT OF THE COUNTRY AND HE DIDN'T EXACTLY LEAVE THINGS IN PERFECT HEALTH.
NOT TO MENTION, I'M HAVING TROUBLE KEEPING MY PEOPLE IN THE SAME STATE OF SUSPENDED TERROR THAT HE SEEMED TO.

THE PERILS OF CORPORATE AMERICA. FASCINATING STUFF, LARRY.
NOW, IF YOU DON'T MIND, I'VE GOT TO CHECK IN WITH A USELESS TASK FORCE TRYING AND FAILING TO GET A GRIP ON --
TUCKER...
... I KNOW THIS IS AWKWARD. I ALSO KNOW I MAY BE TRADING ON OUR RELATIONSHIP HERE...
WHAT RELATIONSHIP? THINGS GOT WEIRD. YOU ENDED IT. SO I ASSUME YOU'RE HERE ON BUSINESS...

SORT OF.
MY CFO IS MISSING. BUT I GOT A TIP THAT HE MIGHT BE SPENDING HIS TIME IN SOME... DISREPUTABLE PLACES. I NEED TO TRY AND GET HIM BACK IN THE SADDLE.
BUT I NEED TO DO IT QUIETLY.
CAN YOU HELP ME?

YOU GOTTA HELP ME OUT A LITTLE, KIDDO...
... WHAT THE HELL AM I SUPPOSED TO DO WITH YOU...?!

NOW, YOU BEST BELIEVE THIS IS A FUCKED UP WORLD YOU GOT SQUEEZED OUT INTO. AND YOU GOT NO PROTECTIONS.
I AIN'T EQUIPPED FOR THIS. I AIN'T GOT ME A POT TO PISS IN OR A WINDOW TO THROW IT OUT OF...

... THING IS, I AIN'T SURE WHAT WE'RE HIDIN' FROM.
WE'RE HIDIN' FROM SOMETHING, THAT'S FOR SURE...

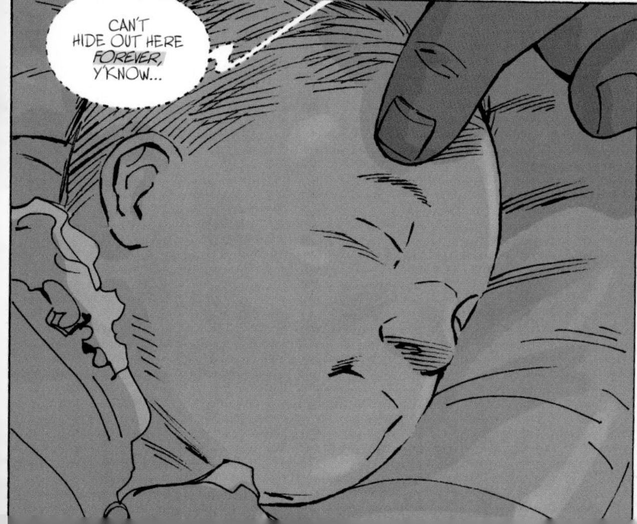
CAN'T HIDE OUT HERE FOREVER, Y'KNOW...

MISS LAGRAVENESE!
WE'VE GOT A... WELL... A SITUATION --
WHAT...?

... I WENT IN YOUR OFFICE TO FILE SOME RECEIPTS AND THERE HE WAS. SCARED THE LIVING SHIT OUT OF ME...!

DID HE TRY TO HURT YOU?

NO, I DON'T THINK HE'S IN ANY CONDITION TO CAUSE THAT KIND OF TROUBLE.
SHOULD I CALL SECURITY TO --
HOLD OFF ON THAT FOR NOW, RACHEL...

... JUST LET ME SEE WHAT WE'RE DEALING WITH FIRST.
OH, FOR CHRISSAKES...

... NICE OF YOU TO DROP IN, CHA CHA.
BY ALL MEANS, MAKE YOURSELF AT HOME...!

CHAPTER THIRTY-NINE

THE RIOT TO ROCK

CHAPTER THIRTY-NINE

THE RIOT TO ROCK

knew this was a bad idea going. But I couldn't help myself. I d to have the conversation.
I UNDERSTAND YOU'RE IN A BAD STATE OF MIND, K.
BUT I WARNED YOU ABOUT SHIT LIKE THIS...

... A BREAK AN'T OPERATE WHEN HE'S CARRYING EMOTIONAL BAGGAGE.
I REMEMBER.
BUT THIS THING WITH THE SKINS... I'VE BEEN ON THE FRONT LINES FOR WEEKS NOW.
WE'RE CLOSE TO WINNING THIS GODDAMN TURF WAR BECAUSE I --
HOLD UP NOW, KEENAN WADE. DON'T START MAKING SOME SPEECH ABOUT YOUR ROLE IN ALL THIS.
AND I THINK "TURF WAR" IS UNDERSELLING WHAT WE'RE DOING HERE...

. WE'RE GONNA KE THIS CITY.
HELL, IT'S ALREADY OURS, AS FAR AS I'M CONCERNED. THEY JUST DON'T KNOW IT YET.
MY GIRL WAS TARGETED, OKAY? THEY WANT ME SO BAD... I'M ASKING YOU TO LET ME TAKE BULLCHUCK DOWN ONCE AND FOR ALL.

NO...
... I DON'T THINK SO.

THAT AIN'T THE RIGHT MOVE FOR US.
Tough to hide my disbelief when I hear Masai pronounce his judgment. I still want my revenge.

WAIT!
YOU CAN'T --
DON'T RAISE YOUR VOICE TO ME, BOY. YOU CAN'T EXPECT TO IGNORE MY COUNSEL AND THEN TALK ME INTO SOMETHING I DON'T BELIEVE IN...!
DUE RESPECT, MASAI, BUT YOU DON'T 'BELIEVE' IN IT?!
OUR ENTIRE WAY OF LIFE IS BASED ON EYE-FOR-AN-EYE!
THAT'S RIGHT.
BUT IF WE'RE GONNA TRULY ASCEND, THEN IT'S UP TO US TO RISE ABOVE THAT BRAND OF BLOODLUST.
THAT'S WHAT MAKES US BETTER THAN THE SKINS.
NOW, IF YOU'VE GOT DIFFERENT IDEAS ABOUT HOW THINGS SHOULD GO, YOU BEST THINK AGAIN...

... BECAUSE YOU AIN'T THE ONE RUNNIN' THE SHOW, ARE YOU?
And there it is. The demonstration of muscle. The implied threat.
YOU KNOW WHAT HAPPENS TO THE FOOLS WHO STEP TO ME...
... SHIT DON'T END WELL.
The message he's sending is clear. Swallow my fire. Fall in line or else.

THE AUSTRIAN ALPS:
WE ARE THE FULFILLMENT OF MANKIND'S *PROMISE*...

... WHAT HAS BEEN *DISCUSSED* HERE -- AMONGST THIS BROTHERHOOD OF LUMINARIES -- WILL ALLOW US TO MORE ACCURATELY SURVEY THE CIVILIZED WORLD.
WE ALL *KNOW* WHAT WE SEE THERE --

-- WE SEE *OPPORTUNITY*. WE SEE *POWER*. WE SEE THE *NEW* WORLD.
THE SYMBOLS AND CEREMONIES WE INDULGE IN SERVE TO PROVE THAT ONLY *MAN* CAN FULLY CONTROL HIS ENVIRONMENT.
WE WILL ALL PLAY A PART IN *SHAPING* THAT ENVIRONMENT. WE HAVE *EARNED* OUR IMMORTALITY...

... BUT FOR NOW, WE SHOULD *EMBRACE* OUR HUMANITY. WE SHOULD *CELEBRATE* IT.
WE SHOULD LOOK EACH OTHER IN THE EYE AND *ACCEPT* OUR ASCENSION...
... TO THAT HIGHER PLACE.
WE WILL EXCEED OUR REACH... OR WHAT'S A HEAVEN FOR?

HE CERTAINLY KNOWS HOW TO PUT THINGS INTO PERSPECTIVE, DOESN'T HE...?
IT'S ALL A BIT OF *SHOW BUSINESS*, EH?
WELL, LIGETI'S A TRADITIONALIST... MAYBE A LITTLE SUPERSTITIOUS, TOO...

... WHAT ABOUT *YOU*, MISTER COOKE? I HEAR THIS IS YOUR FIRST MEETING.
WHAT DO YOU THINK?

I THINK... I'D WANT TO KNOW MORE ABOUT THE *ENDGAME*.
IT'S *BEYOND* THE CONCEPT OF GLOBAL GOVERNMENT --

-- THAT'S TOO *SIMPLE*. ACKNOWLEDGING THE WORLD BANK'S INFLUENCE? FAR TOO PAT.
SOMEONE'S GOT TO MAKE SURE WE'RE HEADED IN THE RIGHT DIRECTION.
WHO'S MORE *QUALIFIED*...?

GOOD QUESTION --
NOW WE SHIFT INTO THAT SATISFIED STATE...

... ONE WHERE WE REVEL WITH AS MUCH FERVOR AS WE WORK.
AS OUR INFLUENCE IS FELT, WE LEAVE OUR CARES BEHIND.
AT LEAST FOR TONIGHT...
... FOR THIS PURPOSE, WE HAVE MADE SPECIAL ARRANGEMENTS.
SO INDULGE AND ENJOY.
LET YOUR NEEDS BE FULLY MET AND YOUR HEADS FULLY CLEARED.
FLESH MUST BE FED. AND FED WELL.
NOW GO FORTH AND CONQUER.
THAT'S OUR CUE...
HEARD SOME GOOD THINGS ABOUT THIS YEAR'S CROP.
YOU BETTER GET IN ON THIS, COOKE. PUT A LITTLE HAIR ON YOUR CHEST...

HNN!
MMM...?
OHHH... SHIT! I WAS JUST --
CHRIST... FREEZING OUT HERE...!

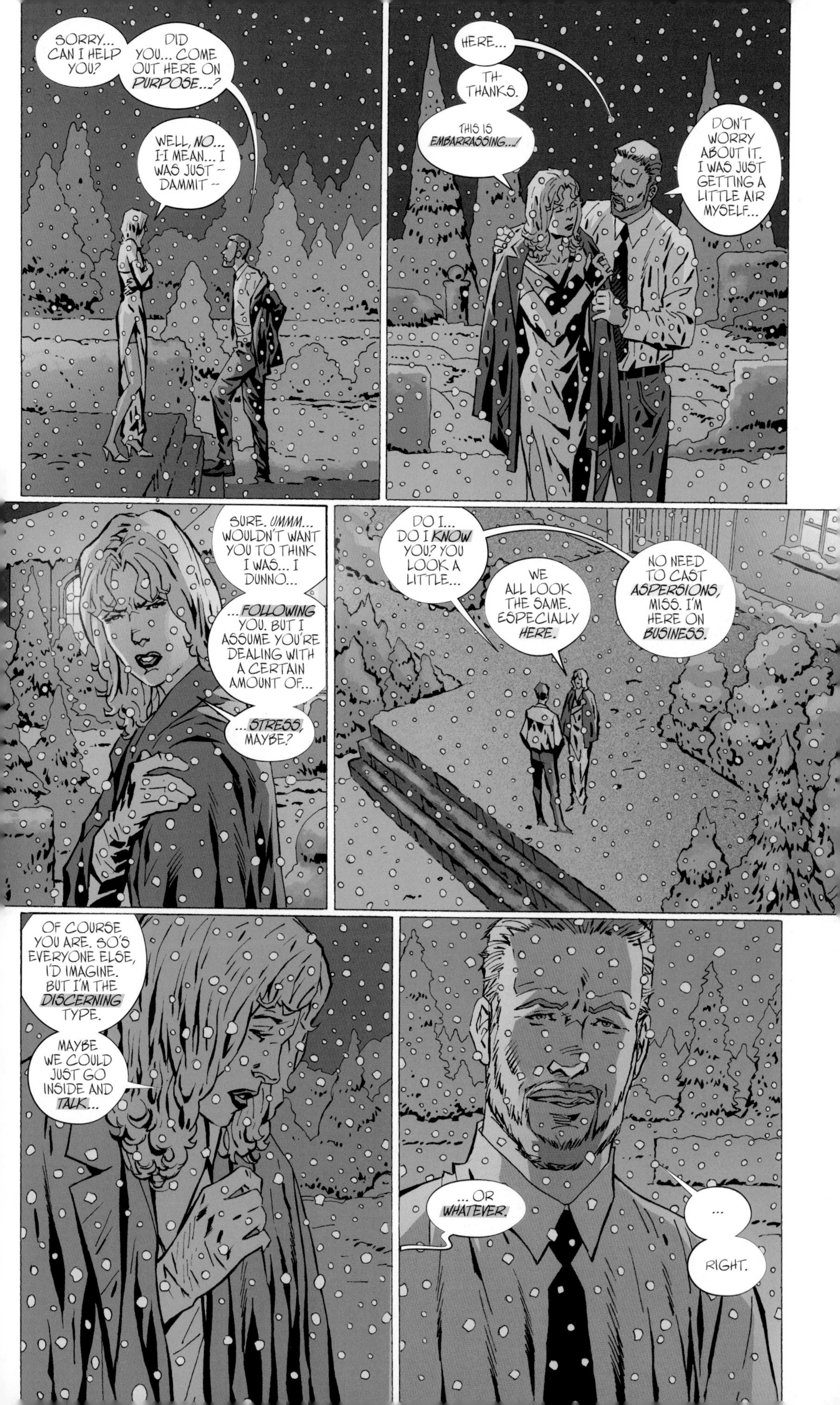
SORRY... CAN I HELP YOU?
DID YOU... COME OUT HERE ON PURPOSE...?
WELL, NO... I-I MEAN... I WAS JUST -- DAMMIT --
HERE...
TH- THANKS.
THIS IS EMBARRASSING...!
DON'T WORRY ABOUT IT. I WAS JUST GETTING A LITTLE AIR MYSELF...
SURE. UMMM... WOULDN'T WANT YOU TO THINK I WAS... I DUNNO...
...FOLLOWING YOU. BUT I ASSUME YOU'RE DEALING WITH A CERTAIN AMOUNT OF...
...STRESS, MAYBE?
DO I... DO I KNOW YOU? YOU LOOK A LITTLE...
WE ALL LOOK THE SAME. ESPECIALLY HERE.
NO NEED TO CAST ASPERSIONS, MISS. I'M HERE ON BUSINESS.
OF COURSE YOU ARE. SO'S EVERYONE ELSE, I'D IMAGINE. BUT I'M THE DISCERNING TYPE.
MAYBE WE COULD JUST GO INSIDE AND TALK...
...OR WHATEVER.
...
RIGHT.

... SO WHEN DID YOU ALL ARRIVE?
YESTERDAY. WE HAD TO TAKE SNOWCATS TO GET HERE.
QUITE A RIDE.
I'LL BET.
IN THIS WEATHER, I THINK THEY'LL PROBABLY HAVE TO HELICOPTER US OUT OF HERE.
YOU'RE STILL SHAKING. YOU CAN KEEP THE COAT ON...
NO, IT'S OKAY...

... BESIDES, IT'D BE A REAL SHAME TO KEEP THIS OUTFIT COVERED UP.
WE GO TO A LOT OF... WELL... EFFORT TO MAKE SURE YOU'RE ALL... SATISFIED. ALTHOUGH... AHEM! ... IT'S OUR PLEASURE.
YOU CERTAINLY SEEM LIKE A MAN WHO COULD USE A LITTLE --
LET ME STOP YOU RIGHT THERE.
I'M WELL AWARE OF THE DYNAMIC INVOLVED WHEN IT COMES TO... THIS LITTLE INTERACTION.
AND I KNOW WHAT'S EXPECTED OF YOU.
YOUR... SUBTLE PROPOSITIONS NOTWITHSTANDING, I'M CONTENT TO LET THE REST OF THEM BELIEVE WE SHOOK THE PILLARS IN HERE. THAT'S THE IDEA, RIGHT?
NO NEED TO ACTUALLY FOLLOW THROUGH WITH IT.
SO YOU CAN SAVE THE SALES PITCH.
WELL, THAT'S...
OKAY.
THEN... NOW WHAT...?

NOW... WE HAVE OURSELVES A DRINK.
I MEAN, WE WANT TO KEEP UP APPEARANCES, DON'T WE?

I'M SURE WE BOTH HAVE REPUTATIONS TO UPHOLD IN THESE HEIGHTENED CIRCUMSTANCES.
WELL... AS LONG AS YOU'RE HAPPY, I GUESS.
YOU MUST BE AN OLD HAND AT THESE MEETINGS.

I WOULDN'T SAY THAT, EXACTLY.
JUST LIKE I WOULDN'T SAY YOU'RE A BONA FIDE WORKING GIRL...

...ARE YOU?
I, UUHHH... I'M NOT SURE WHAT YOU...
I MEAN, I'M HERE TO... YOU KNOW...
...T-TAKE CARE OF YOU.

TAKE A BREATH, OKAY? MAYBE WE SHOULD JUST START OVER.
WHOEVER YOU ARE... YOU'RE PROBABLY CURIOUS ABOUT THIS WHOLE ROTHCHILD THING...?
SHIT.
YOU'RE... NOT GOING TO SEND ME AWAY, ARE YOU?

WELL...
...THAT ALL DEPENDS.

I'M STILL NOT SURE WHY YOU NEED *ME* FOR THIS...
SATURN CITY:

... HAVE YOU EVER BEEN TO THIS GUY'S APARTMENT BEFORE?
NEVER.
LOOK... THIS IS JUST A WEIRD SITUATION ALL AROUND.
THE WAY ELLIOT'S BEEN *ACTING* -- EVEN *BEFORE* HE WENT AWOL -- I CAN'T BE SURE *WHAT* WE'LL FIND HERE.

I'VE NEVER EVEN MET HIS *WIFE*...
WELL, NO ONE'S ANSWERING. MAYBE *SHE* WENT AWOL, TOO...
YOU STILL WANT *IN?* SPREAD OUT FOR A SEC --

-- *I'LL* GET US IN!

JEEZUS, TUCKER...!
OH MY GOD. WHAT *HAPPENED* IN HERE?!
I DUNNO... I'VE NEVER BEEN MARRIED.
BUT THIS IS EXACTLY HOW I ALWAYS *PICTURED* IT.

VERY FUNNY.
YOU TRYING TO *TELL* ME SOMETHING THERE...?

THAT DEPENDS, I GUESS.
TWO PEOPLE TRYING TO MAKE IT WORK... QUITE AN UNDERTAKING.
CLEARLY I'M NO EXPERT ON RELATIONSHIPS --
OH, COME ON --

-- I DIDN'T ASK FOR YOUR HELP SO WE COULD REHASH... WELL, US.
IF IT MAKES ANY DIFFERENCE, I'M JUST AS BAD AT THIS AS YOU THINK YOU ARE.

BUT JUST BECAUSE I SHOULDER MOST OF THE BLAME DOESN'T MEAN WE SHOULDN'T HAVE ENDED IT.
LET'S JUST FINISH LOOKING AROUND AND GET OUT QUICK.
I'LL CHECK THE BEDROOMS.

HELLO? ANYONE IN...
... HERE...?
OH CHRIST...!

M-MISS BARNES...?
...NNNNNNNNN...

I'M NOT SURE WHY WE GET ALL THE STRAYS...

... BUT SOMEHOW THEY JUST KEEP SHOWING UP.
YOU GUYS HAVE BEEN SQUATTING IN, WHERE, THE PLUSH LOUNGE...?
IS THAT WHAT IT'S CALLED? LOTTA PILLOWS IN THERE...

LISTEN... I KNOW MISS LAGRAVENESE IS RUNNIN' A BUSINESS HERE. A REAL SKIN TRADE.
I KEEP THIS LIL' GUY FAR AWAY FROM THAT SHIT...

WELL... CAN I HOLD HIM...?
NAH, I DON'T THINK SO.
HE DON'T LIKE STRANGERS...

... HE JUST LIKES BEING HELD MY ME.
AIN'T THAT RIGHT, KIDDO...?

PANT
PANT
GUH
TAKE IT EASY, CHA CHA...

ANOTHER ATTEMPT TO GET ME TO *THROW IN* WITH YOU AND YOUR BROTHER...
M-MY *BROTHER*... HE MUST BE... SO COMPLETELY *FUCKED*...!
SO?
I'LL ADMIT, IT'S A LITTLE UNNERVING TO SEE YOU *NOT* FUSED TO DOLPH'S HIP. THE FACT THAT YOU CAME *HERE* FOR SANCTUARY...

...YOU WANT TO FILL ME IN ON WHAT'S UP?
I DUNNO... I DUNNO... IF THEY'VE *GOT* HIM... THEN THAT MEANS... *SH-SHIT*...

MISS LAGRAVENESE...
...EVERYTHING *ALRIGHT* IN HERE?
ONE SECOND, CHA CHA...
NF

WHAT'S UP?
WELL, I JUST WANTED TO *REMIND* YOU THAT WE'VE GOT CLIENTS -- *REGULARS* -- WAITING FOR THIS ROOM *AND* THE PLUSH LOUNGE...
I KNOW. AND I CERTAINLY DON'T NEED *THIS* ADDED AGGRAVATION. FIRST THINGS FIRST...

...LET'S FIGURE OUT WHERE TO STASH *THIS* ONE --
GAAAH--!
HNNNGGKK!

WHAT'D YOU DO?!
F-FUCK ME... IT HURTS...
ME? NOT A GODDAMN THING...!
BUT THE WAY HE'S BREAKING DOWN... SOMEONE DID A NUMBER ON HIM...!

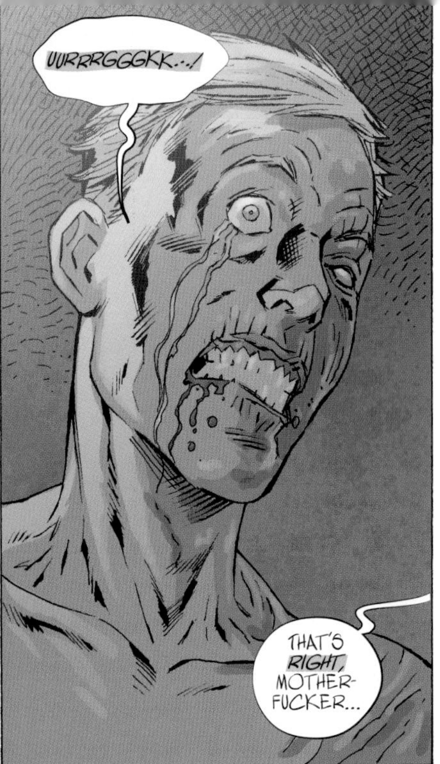
UURRRGGGKK...!
THAT'S RIGHT, MOTHER-FUCKER...

... SUCKS TO BE YOU, DON'T IT?
LOOK AT HIM, RAY. THIS CRACKER'S PETRIFIED...!
GOOD ONE, REGGIE --

-- BUT HE AIN'T BEEN TAKEN TO THE LIMIT. NOT YET, ANYWAY.
... NGGGG...
... F-F-FGGG... YYYY...
FUCK ME?! NAH, MAN... I AIN'T FEELIN' NO PAIN. I KNOW YOU FEEL THAT SHIT...

... RIGHT DOWN TO YOUR BONES.

GET OVER THERE, GIRL. GIVE HIM ANOTHER TASTE...
SURE THING...
... IF, FOR NO OTHER REASON, TO MAKE UP FOR NOT GETTING BOTH OF THEM.
THEN AGAIN... MAYBE I DIDN'T HAVE TO. MAYBE THERE'S SOMETHING MORE HERE THAN JUST TWO BROTHERS AND THEIR SHARED SENSE OF FASHION...

DON'T FORGET ABOUT THEIR DELUSIONS OF GRANDEUR.
OH, AIN'T NO ONE FORGETTIN' ABOUT THAT. ESPECIALLY NOT THE OLD MAN.
HE GAVE US STRICT INSTRUCTIONS, Y'DIG?

THIS IS JUST THE FIRST STEP IN STOPPIN' THEIR SHIT COLD.
SO THIS ONE'S... DOLPH, RIGHT...?
WHAT'S THE DIFFERENCE? OUR SECRET WEAPON'S GOT HERSELF A HUNCH AND I'M INCLINED TO BUY INTO IT. IF YOU'VE GOT ONE OF 'EM ...
... YOU'VE GOT A DIRECT LINE TO THE OTHER.
WHAT COMES NEXT... THINK OF IT AS SENDING A SPECIFIC MESSAGE.
THE REST OF THEM WILL GET THEIRS IN TIME. BUT FOR NOW...
... I'LL JUST FOCUS ON YOU.
--HHURRGGAAAHH--!

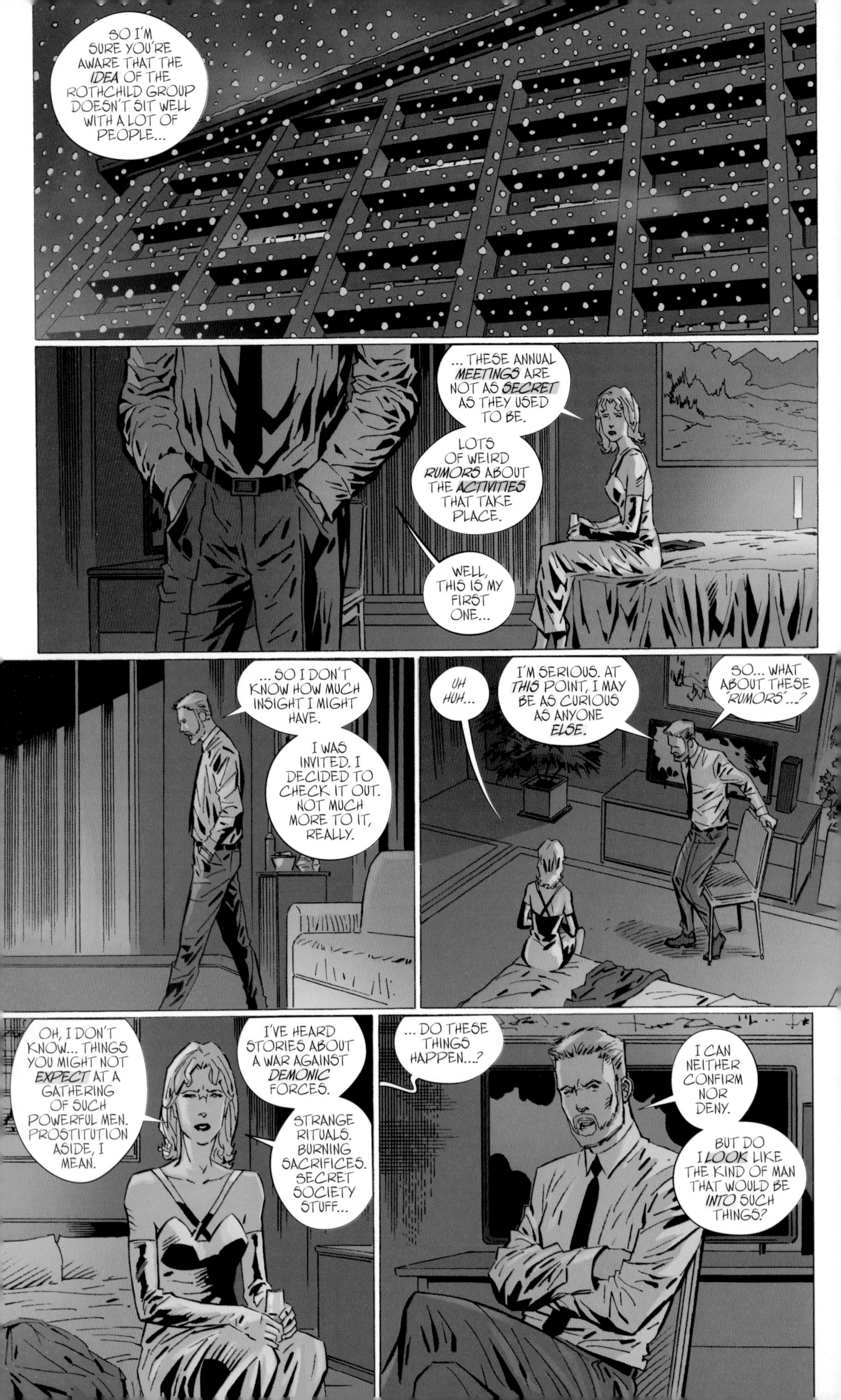
SO I'M SURE YOU'RE AWARE THAT THE IDEA OF THE ROTHCHILD GROUP DOESN'T SIT WELL WITH A LOT OF PEOPLE...
... THESE ANNUAL MEETINGS ARE NOT AS SECRET AS THEY USED TO BE.
LOTS OF WEIRD RUMORS ABOUT THE ACTIVITIES THAT TAKE PLACE.
WELL, THIS IS MY FIRST ONE...
... SO I DON'T KNOW HOW MUCH INSIGHT I MIGHT HAVE.
I WAS INVITED. I DECIDED TO CHECK IT OUT. NOT MUCH MORE TO IT, REALLY.
UH HUH...
I'M SERIOUS. AT THIS POINT, I MAY BE AS CURIOUS AS ANYONE ELSE.
SO... WHAT ABOUT THESE "RUMORS"...?
OH, I DON'T KNOW... THINGS YOU MIGHT NOT EXPECT AT A GATHERING OF SUCH POWERFUL MEN. PROSTITUTION ASIDE, I MEAN.
I'VE HEARD STORIES ABOUT A WAR AGAINST DEMONIC FORCES.
STRANGE RITUALS. BURNING SACRIFICES. SECRET SOCIETY STUFF...
... DO THESE THINGS HAPPEN...?
I CAN NEITHER CONFIRM NOR DENY.
BUT DO I LOOK LIKE THE KIND OF MAN THAT WOULD BE INTO SUCH THINGS?

THAT IS AN EXCELLENT QUESTION. WHAT KIND OF MAN ARE YOU?
YOU'RE IMPORTANT, AT LEAST. IMPORTANT ENOUGH TO BE INVITED HERE.

YOU'RE RICH AND YOU'RE WHITE. THAT STILL SCORES A LOT OF POINTS THESE DAYS.
ALTHOUGH I IMAGINE YOU STILL LIVE A VERY... CONSTRUCTED LIFE...

... YOU SAID IT YOURSELF, YOU'RE BIG ON APPEARANCES. YOU WANT TO BE VIEWED IN A CERTAIN WAY.
WHETHER IT'S SOCIALLY OR POLITICALLY... IT'S ALL ABOUT MAINTAINING THE FACADE, AM I RIGHT...?

LIKE I SAID...
... I CAN NEITHER CONFIRM NOR DENY.
BUT IT SOUNDS... EXHAUSTING, DOESN'T IT?

THIS TYPE OF GATHERING BRINGS WITH IT... A KIND OF CERTAINTY.
POWER AND PRIVILEGE. THESE THINGS COME AT A PRICE...

... ALONG WITH ITS FAIR SHARE OF HUBRIS.
IS THAT A CONDEMNATION?

ISN'T THAT WHAT WE'RE ALL ABOUT?
WE LIVE. WE SEE. WE JUDGE.
AND THEN WE ACT.

ACTING AS OUR SAVIORS, YOU MEAN? WHO ASKED YOU?
YOU'RE RIGHT... NO ONE ASKED ME.
THE PROBLEM IS... MOST PEOPLE AREN'T EVEN AWARE OF THE QUESTION.

OKAY, THAT ONE'S TOUGH TO ARGUE.
YOU THINK ORDINARY PEOPLE CAN'T HANDLE THE TRUTH?

WELL, TELL YOU WHAT... YOU DEFINE "TRUTH" FOR ME AND I'LL LET YOU KNOW.
WHILE YOU'RE AT IT, DEFINE "ORDINARY", TOO.
IN THE MEANTIME, SOMETHING JUST OCCURRED TO ME...

... DESPITE THE PRETENSE, I'M STARTING TO HAVE... THOUGHTS.
WE DON'T KNOW EACH OTHER, DO WE? WE'RE TOTAL STRANGERS HERE...
THAT'S... RIGHT, I SUPPOSE.

WELL, IN THAT SPIRIT...
... MAYBE WE SHOULD TAKE SOME ADVANTAGE OF THIS CIRCUMSTANCE.
UMMM...
... WHAT...?

TAKE... ADVANTAGE? B-BUT I THOUGHT...
OH...
... YOU'RE... JUST GOING AHEAD WITH IT...

L-LOOK, I'M NOT SURE IF...
... THIS IS A GOOD IDEA...
YOU KNOW, YOU'RE VERY INTUITIVE.

THE QUESTIONS YOU ASK... I DON'T USUALLY SUBMIT MYSELF TO ANY KIND OF INTERROGATION...
I... UUHHH... I DUNNO...
YOU DON'T...?
... W-WELL, I MEAN... IT FEELS LIKE...

... AAHHH... ARE YOU S-SURE THAT --
DON'T WORRY. I'M PRETTY GOOD AT THIS...
... I KNOW ALL THE RIGHT...

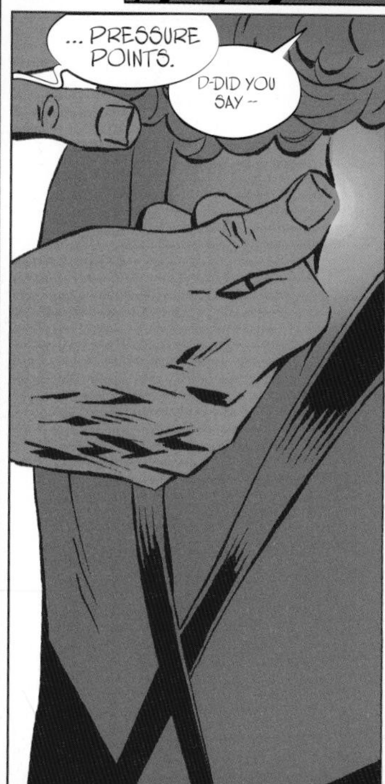
... PRESSURE POINTS.
D-DID YOU SAY --

-- PRESSURE...?
... MMM...

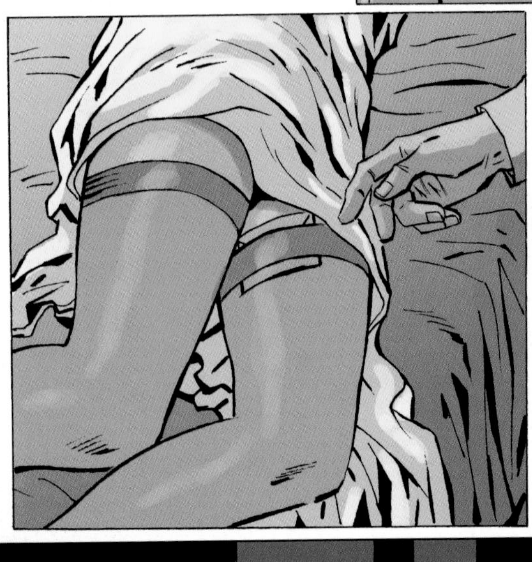

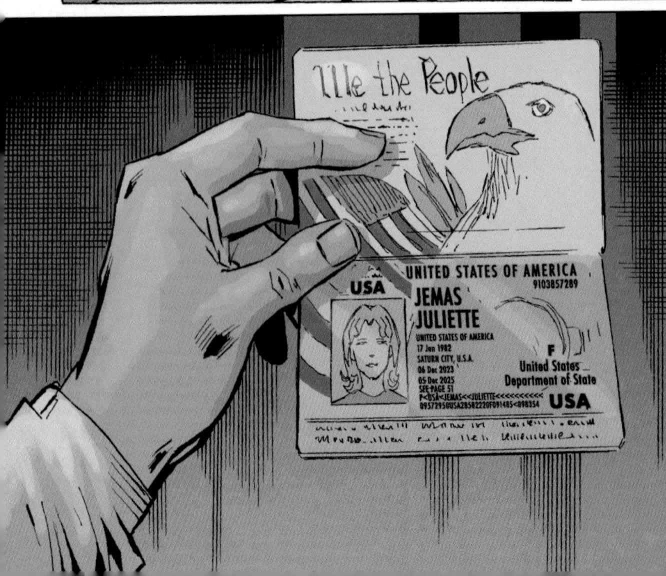

We the People
UNITED STATES OF AMERICA
9103857289
USA
JEMAS
JULIETTE
UNITED STATES OF AMERICA
17 Jun 1982
SATURN CITY, U.S.A.
F
United States
Department of State
USA

SIGH
RIGHT.

CENTERLAND TERMINAL:
... THE COAST GUARD ACTUALLY LET THIS BIG OL' BOAT PASS WITHOUT INSPECTION?
MAYBE ON PURPOSE. THESE DAYS, YOU NEVER KNOW WHO'S ON THE TAKE...

... LET'S FIND OUT WHAT THIS TUB IS HAULING THAT'S SO GODDAMN IMPORTANT.
OH SHIT. CHECK THIS OUT --
-- SOMEONE WAS MAKING A COZY LITTLE HOME DOWN HERE...!
NOT ONLY THAT --

-- LOOKS LIKE THEY'VE KEPT THEMSELVES FED ON A HEALTHY DIET OF VERMIN AND GOD KNOWS WHAT ELSE...!

STOWAWAYS AREN'T UNCOMMON ON THESE CARGO SHIPS, RIGHT...?
DEPENDS.
LET'S TRY TO SUSS OUT THE CREW... SEE WHAT THE FUCK THEY MIGHT KNOW...

... HE SAYS HE DOESN'T KNOW THE PORT OF ORIGIN.
WELL, THAT'S JUST FUCKING GREAT. CAN ANYONE PRODUCE SOME KIND OF MANIFEST, AT LEAST?
I WOULDN'T COUNT ON IT. EVEN HIS DIALECT IS A LITTLE OFF...
SHOULD WE GET THE N.I.C.E.* GUYS DOWN HERE...?
ARE YOU KIDDING? THEY NEVER COME TO SATURN...!
WELL, SOMEBODY JUST SNUCK INTO OUR CITY...
* National Immigration and Customs Enforceme

... AND WE'RE NOT GONNA KNOW JACK-SHIT UNTIL THEY DO WHATEVER THEY CAME HERE TO DO.

SSNNNFFF
OH YEAH. I KNOW THIS SMELL...

... THE HEADY SMELL OF COMPLETE SOCIAL DECAY.
FEELS GOOD TO BE BACK HOME.

TO BE CONTINUED

BOOK SEVEN

CRISIS APOCALYPTO

JOE CASEY & PIOTR KOWALSKI

WITH BRAD SIMPSON · RUS WOOTON · SONIA HARRIS

OTHER WORKS BY JOE CASEY

CODEFLESH WITH CHARLIE ADLARD

ROCK BOTTOM WITH CHARLIE ADLARD

KRASH BASTARDS WITH AXEL 13

NIXON'S PALS WITH CHRIS BURNHAM

OFFICER DOWNE WITH CHRIS BURNHAM

CHARLATAN BALL WITH ANDY SURIANO

DOC BIZARRE, M.D. WITH ANDY SURIANO

THE MILKMAN MURDERS WITH STEVE PARKHOUSE

FULL MOON FEVER WITH CALEB GERARD/DAMIAN COUCEIRO

BUTCHER BAKER THE RIGHTEOUS MAKER
WITH MIKE HUDDLESTON

THE BOUNCE WITH DAVID MESSINA & SONIA HARRIS

GØDLAND WITH TOM SCIOLI

VALHALLA MAD WITH PAUL MAYBURY

ANNUAL WITH LUKE PARKER, SONIA HARRIS & VARIOUS

NEW LIEUTENANTS OF METAL WITH ULISES FARINAS

MCMLXXV WITH IAN MACEWAN

JESUSFREAK WITH BENJAMIN MARRA

THE
BOUNCE

THE FUTURE OF COMICS
25
EST. 1992
ANNUAL
2017
$9.99
1st Edition

JESUSFREAK
JOE
CASEY
BENJAMIN
MARRA

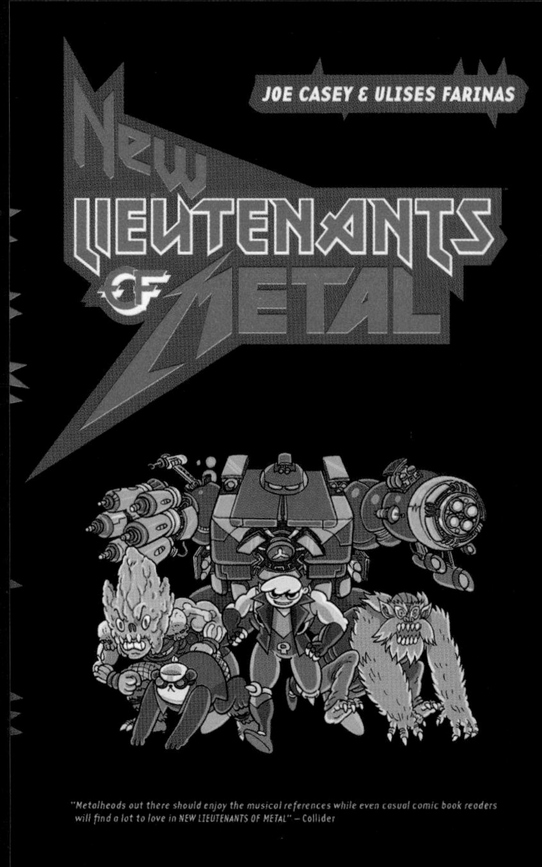
JOE CASEY & ULISES FARINAS
New
LIEUTENANTS
OF METAL
"Metalheads out there should enjoy the musical references while even casual comic book readers will find a lot to love in NEW LIEUTENANTS OF METAL" – Collider